W9-BYK-907

For the Best in Literature

PO/NT

Fallen Angels
Walter Dean Myers

Slam!
Walter Dean Myers

From the Notebooks of Melanin Sun
Jacqueline Woodson

Make Lemonade
Virginia Euwer Wolff

My Brother Sam Is Dead
James Lincoln Collier and Christopher Collier

Plain City
Virginia Hamilton

Toning the Sweep
Angela Johnson

When She Hollers
Cynthia Voigt

When She Was Good
Norma Fox Mazer

Shadow of the Red Moon

WALTER DEAN MYERS

Illustrations by Christopher Myers

SCHOLASTIC INC.

New York   Toronto   London   Auckland   Sydney
Mexico City   New Delhi   Hong Kong   Buenos Aires

No part of this publication may be reproduced in whole or in part, or stored in a retrieval system, or transmitted in any form or by any means, electronic, mechanical, photocopying, recording, or otherwise, without written permission of the publisher. For information regarding permission, write to Scholastic Inc., Attn: Permissions Dept., 557 Broadway, New York, NY, 10012

ISBN 0-439-63616-7

12 11 10 9 8 7 6 5 4 3 2   4 5 6 7 8 9/0

Printed in the U.S.A.   01

Shadow of the Red Moon

PROLOGUE

This is the story of a people. They call themselves Okalians, which means "The People Who Dream Greatly." The Okalians trace their history back to a time when stories were not written, but passed from generation to generation by word of mouth. Eventually they came to write their story in the Book of Orenllag. The Book became the legend of their triumph, their rise to greatness. It was the truth as they knew it to be, and the truth by which they would try to live.

They had settled in the southern part of the land, where the sea formed a protective border and the foods were plentiful. Here they lived in peace and security for tens upon tens of generations. Then came the calamity, which, according to their own legend, was one of the trials that proved their greatness.

There had been first a great disturbance in the sky. The rains poured heavily for six days and lightning ripped across the horizon like the brilliant fingers of an angry god. Some said they saw the meteor when it first appeared, others saw it only after it had broken into a thousand smaller meteors burning in the night air before crashing heavily to the ground, lifting a great black cloud that rose many times higher than the mountains. The entire sky darkened with the thick, choking dust and all the world was plunged into a numbing cold. All living creatures suffered. It was then that the Okalians were forced to leave their homes and journey across the Wilderness looking for a place free from the settling dust, where they could begin to build and to renew their lives.

When they found this higher ground, this place of new beginning, they built a city whose walls were made of solid crystal. The crystals held what little sunlight filtered through the dust and made life bearable. Even though this Crystal City, as they called it, was a wondrous invention, life for the Okalians had still been hard. But they had survived, and in their surviving had become stronger and more convinced of their greatness.

The dust eventually grew less dense and the world began to warm. They saw that a New Moon had appeared in the distance. Unlike the Red Moon they had always known, the New Moon seemed cold and menacing. Some saw it as a good sign and thought it was the omen of a new prosperity, a new tranquility. But with the warming of the world came the great plague.

The Okalians, behind the protective walls of Crystal City, were not affected by the plague, but were witness to its terrible effect. Whoever was exposed to the plague, with few exceptions, was struck down between the sixteenth and seventeenth year, creating in the Wilderness a world composed almost completely of children. When this was discovered, the Elders in the Crystal City decided to lock their gates and keep out the plague, and all strangers who might bring it into the city were turned away.

Of all the people who once lived in the Wilderness, the Na'ans, the Kargs, and the Fens, the people most affected by the plague were the Fens. Many of the Fen children immediately died of starvation or were killed by roaming bands of wild animals. Only the strongest survived, those almost as wild as the animals that attacked them. The Fen children formed their own society and began to dominate the hard world about them. In the process they wrote no book, but did create their own version of truth and seek their own place in the world. Not finding such a place in the Wilderness, they finally turned their eyes to the Crystal City, the one place that had been closed off to them, that had shut them out.

on was so scared. So scared. They had told him that it was the Okalian children who would save their world, but they didn't tell him anything about how scared he would be. The Fen children had been surrounding Crystal City for months, hurling rocks and stones and sharpened flints, trying to tear their way inside the gleaming walls. Months before, in the middle of the night, they had sent out nearly a hundred Okalian children, who attempted to steal through the Fen camps. But the signal fires they were supposed to light were never seen and no one in Crystal City knew how many, if any, had survived. Now the Fens had made cracks in the walls, and it was only a matter of time before they broke through.

"You are the hope of our people," his father had said. "You last children."

There were only twenty-four Okalian children left in the city. Everyone sixteen and over stayed back to hold off the Fens. The youngest children, those under six, were kept with their families. The others were going out of the tunnels, one by one. It was hoped that the older children and the adults could hold off the Fens long enough for the twenty-four of them to make their way through the ventilating tunnels and into the Wilderness. From there they would have to find a way back to the Ancient Land, to make a new start for the Okalians.

The tunnel was inky dark. Jon couldn't see his hands in front of his face as he edged along the damp wall. There was a slight breeze, cool wind in his face, as he neared the opening that led to the grounds outside the tunnel. In the distance he could hear noises. He imagined what they would be. Sounds of battle? Sounds of people crying out in agony? Don't think, he told himself. Just get to the entrance to the tunnel.

He sucked in as much cool air as he could as he reached the grating that covered the tunnel.

He pushed on the grating. At first it didn't move, and he panicked. He didn't want to be trapped in the tunnel, to have the Fens find him there. He clenched his teeth and pushed with all of his strength. One side of the grating gave way and then the other. He pushed it aside and climbed out. He was on his hands and knees. The ground was wet and icy cold. He crawled forward, lifting his head, squinting his eyes.

He remembered that there were two hundred and sixty paces between the walls of Crystal City and the first stand of trees. Pushing himself to his feet, he tried to remember in what direction the trees were.

For a moment an image of his mother came to him. It was the look on her face as she watched him go through the door for the last time. The noises of the fighters had been getting louder and louder. He had been so scared. There was such a terrible look in her eyes, such a desperate, terrible look. They were losing each other and they both knew it.

"It is only our children who can save us," his father had said. "They are the ones who must carry our dreams."

Jon wiped quickly at the tears in his eyes and started forward. Just as he spotted the trees a torch flared to his left. The Fens were starting fires near the tunnels. Jon dove to the ground. A sharp pain ripped through his knees and he clenched his fists tightly to keep from crying out. From somewhere in the darkness there were screams and shouting. The Fens had found the tunnels and were attacking them.

The noises, the cries, seemed to come from everywhere. Jon looked back toward the tunnel. He saw, or he thought he saw, shadows moving behind him. He forced himself to crawl forward for a while, then to stand and run as fast as he could toward the darkness of the trees. Behind him an alarm clanged noisily, drowning out all other sounds. The outer walls had been penetrated. The Fens were in Crystal City!

He reached the first line of trees and went on, stumbling through the darkness, his breath coming in short, rasping gasps, his knees aching, the low tree limbs tearing his face in the darkness. His heart pounded wildly and small whimpering sounds came from his throat.

He kept running away from Crystal City. He ran until he couldn't run anymore, until his body screamed with pain and his legs, heavy with fatigue, just stopped moving. Ahead of him he saw the outline of a gnarled tree, its petrified branches splintered and twisted as they had been for a hundred years. He pulled himself into it, climbed as high as he could, and clung desperately to the thick trunk. He looked back toward Crystal City and saw it surrounded by the flickering lights of a hundred torches bobbing in the night.

He clung to the tree limb with all his might. He thought about his mother again. He had been glad to leave when he heard the sounds of the battle. For all of her heartbreak and his father's talk about being proud of being an Okalian, nothing had mattered to him but how scared he had been, how he had wanted to escape.

He was afraid to stay in the tree, and afraid to let it go. Scenes flashed through his mind. The children sitting together when they were told who was to try to break out, and who was to remain behind.

"Plagues end," the Elder had said. "We don't know if this plague has ended. If it has not ended, then it won't do us any good to have the adults or older children leave the city. You are the ones who are left, and you can save that precious ideal of what it means to be an Okalian."

He hadn't said anything about the Fen children who lived in the Wilderness, who were attacking them.

Jon told himself that he would reach the Ancient Land. That somehow all of the Okalian children would make it there and be safe again. Maybe, he told himself, the Fens would spare the others in Crystal City once they had broken through the walls. He searched himself for hope, for some small comfort he could believe in, but the only thing he could find was his cold cheek against the tree and the awful sense of being more alone than he had ever been. After a long time he fell asleep.

He woke with a start. The sky was barely light, the day a gray, silent veil around him. He looked toward Crystal City. It was farther away than he had thought it would be, but he could still see it through the mist. Fires from the attack still burned. Where the gold and crystal spires had once gleamed, there were curled wisps of black smoke. Even as he watched, another tower crumbled, seeming first to bow, then to lean heavily to one side before finally falling.

"Move." He spoke the word aloud to himself. He had to keep moving.

Each of the children had been given directions to reach the land where the Okalians had first found their greatness. There had been disputes among the elders as to how far away it was, and what dangers lay ahead of them, but with the Fens breaking through their defenses, it was their only hope.

There were no signs of Fens near him. Had they all rushed to the Crystal City? What were they doing there? Don't think, just keep moving.

Jon searched the skies until he found the twin Shan stars. He remembered his mother holding him on her knee when he was a child and pointing them out to him. She made a little rhyme about them, how if he were good they would point to his true love.

"All in due time, of course," she had said, smiling. "All in due time."

He lined up the Shan stars with his hand, pointed to the direction they indicated, and started walking.

He told himself that he wouldn't look back at Crystal City, but he did. Turning, he shielded his eyes with his hand and searched the horizon. A misty fog had already partly concealed the city of his birth. He thought he saw lights still on, but wasn't sure. He had always been taught to celebrate the wonders of the city, and the wonders of being an Okalian who lived there. Now there was a sadness about the distant shapes that seemed less than solid, almost less than real.

They hadn't been given maps, but they had all memorized the Book of Orenllag and the story of how the Okalians had left the Ancient Land after the meteor and the great dust clouds. The book had been started at Orenllag, and had been finished in Crystal City. Jon thought he might add to it when they reached the Ancient Land.

The land was rough, mountainous. He knew he should come to a river soon. There was a ridge ahead of him and he headed for it, going to his knees as he reached it.

He made his way slowly along the rising earth, feeling his feet slip as the crusted ash gave way beneath him. At the top of the ridge he flattened himself before looking over. Below him was a narrow gorge, only half filled with dark water, and a small wooden bridge that crossed it. For a brief moment he felt a sense of joy, glad to find something he had heard about, but had never seen. But the joy quickly changed to horror. For there, sitting to one side of the bridge, was a Fen.

Before the plague, the Fens, according to Okalian history books, had been a hardy people who devoted most of their time to simple survival. Some, his father had said, seemed capable of more advanced living and even some ingenuity, but it was not the rule.

"But . . . ?" Jon had glanced toward where his mother was mending a shirt.

"Your mother has some Fen blood in her," his father had said. "There was a time when we traded with them."

Jon looked down at the Fen guarding the bridge. It was a boy who looked nothing like his mother. His mother was small, and thin, but graceful in every movement. The Fen below

was short and squat. His hair was red, much lighter than Jon's. Most of the Fens had red hair.

Jon was thinking of turning back, looking for another way to cross the river, when something moved in the tall grass to his left. He looked closely and saw two figures. They were dressed as he was, in tunics and pants instead of the animal skins the Fens wore. They were Okalians.

on caught his breath sharply. It was wonderful to see Okalians. Wonderful. He wanted to stand up and shout to them, to scream out that he was there, too. But just a glance at the Fen near the bridge and he knew he didn't dare give away his position.

From where he was, Jon couldn't tell if the Okalians were boys or girls. He looked for a way to signal them, a small stone, something. He looked back to the bridge, and saw that another Fen had neared it. Jon watched the Fen as he moved slowly, carrying what looked like a bundle of sticks. The Fens had short, stocky legs and seemed to rock from side to side as they walked.

He looked back to where the Okalians had been and at first didn't see them. He felt a moment of panic, a moment in which his stomach seemed to clench and his breath stop. Then he saw them again. They had moved a little closer to the bridge and were huddled together behind a wide, gnarled tree. Jon put his hands flat against the ground and started inching his way down the side of the hill.

By the side of the bridge the two Fens were putting branches into a pile.

He looked back toward the Okalians and saw that they were looking right at him. He lifted his hand and waved nervously, keeping a watchful eye out for the Fens.

The girl looked a year, perhaps two years, older then the boy. She nodded and pointed toward the Fens. Her hair was long and black and she had it tied around her head so that from the distance it had been hard for Jon to see that she was a girl. But up close she was very pretty, with large dark eyes that held him in her gaze. The boy with her looked as if he might be her brother.

"My name is Jon." He whispered when he had reached them. "Are you all right?"

"Yes," the girl said.

The boy didn't answer and Jon saw that his face had been badly scratched. A rag had been tied around his waist and Jon thought that the dark stain on it might have been blood.

"We have to try to make it across the bridge," Jon said. "All the routes go that way."

The girl nodded. The boy was on his knees, looking at the Fens. His chest went up and down quickly and Jon could hear him suck in the cold air.

"Can you go first?" the girl asked.

"Y-yes," Jon answered.

He looked down at the Fens and then at the bridge. If they wandered just a little farther away, he thought he could get across the bridge without being caught. He looked back at the girl. She was holding the boy's shoulders, making him look into her eyes. Jon knew the boy was scared. So was he.

He watched the two Fens who guarded the bridge. They had their fire going now, and pushed branches onto it. They had already cleared the area around them and now were moving farther and farther away to gather wood. Jon waited until they were both a distance from the bridge with their backs turned.

He ran as fast as he could, pumping his legs furiously.

Halfway across the long bridge Jon's leg began to cramp up, but he didn't stop until he had reached the far side. He turned around and saw the other two Okalians running across the bridge with the Fens close behind them.

"Come on! Faster!" Jon called to them. He started backing away as they came closer.

The two Okalians ran as fast as they could. The Fens, who had been gaining on them, began to fall back.

When the boy and girl had crossed the bridge, Jon started to run again. He looked over his shoulder and saw that the Fens had stopped once they had crossed the bridge. The three Okalians kept running, the boy and girl close behind Jon, until they had gone past a rock-strewn field and collapsed in a patch of coarse grass. The Fens were nowhere in sight.

Jon sat up, trying to catch his breath. "We can rest here for a minute or two," he called to the girl. His chest was pounding. "Then we'd better move on."

"Go away!" the boy spit the words out angrily. "Go away!"

Jon looked at the boy for a moment, then at the girl as she sat on the ground, her back against a rock.

The girl seemed all right, but the boy was scratched, and maybe wounded. Still, Jon was glad to see both of them.

The coarse grass cut his hands and he had to shift position to get comfortable. The field was nearly flat. They would have to find a place with more shelter, Jon knew. He didn't know where they were, or how far it was from one landmark to the next. He only knew that somewhere in the vast area they called the Wilderness, he would have to find them. When the Okalians had made the long journey from the Ancient Land to the place on which they had built Crystal City, they had crossed all of these places, and had written them down in the Book of Orenllag.

First there would be the Plain of Souls and, somewhere to the west, the Swarm Mountains. There, if anywhere, the water would be pure. There would also be the chance of finding fruit trees. But the first thing they needed to do was to get out of the field they were in.

"I think we should move on," Jon said. "In case the Fens are following us."

The boy looked away. Jon turned and started slowly across the field. It took a few minutes for the girl to catch up with him. The boy was trailing them.

"Is he all right?" Jon asked the girl.

"Yes," she said. Her voice was flat, labored. Up close she looked to be about fourteen, the boy twelve, no older.

"Have you seen other Okalians?" Jon asked them.

"We were in the first group that left," she said. "We were attacked as soon as we left and we split up. Kyra and I stayed together. I haven't seen any of the others since then."

"Have you seen other Fens?"

"Fens, yes," she said. "And dogs."

"Dogs?"

"I think they were dogs," she said. Her voice was husky, and she spoke slowly. "They were strange, though."

"Did I tell you my name was Jon?"

"I'm Lin, my brother is Kyra," she said. "He's had a hard time."

She didn't go on.

They walked across the field, looking back frequently to see if they were being followed. Jon knew that there would be Fens all along their route, and that they would have to be watchful. He wondered what Lin meant when she said her brother had had a hard time.

The Plain of Souls was a long stretch of rolling hills and ravines. There were trees dotted across the landscape, but little greenery. The whole area had once been covered by a thick, gray layer of dust. Now there was some green, some few signs of new life.

The sky above them was a patchwork of reds and golds. In the distance it was darker, almost brown. Jon remembered seeing the sky from Crystal City. It was beautiful when it was safe.

"I don't think they've followed us," Jon said,

stopping near a small plant. "But I think we might be better off if we travel together."

"Why?" Lin asked.

"We can take turns resting and being on guard," Jon said. "And . . . I really don't want to be out here alone."

"Neither do I." Lin stopped a distance from him.

"You look like a Fen." Kyra's face was puffy.

"No, he doesn't." The girl spoke quickly. "It's just that you don't see many Okalians with red hair."

"My mother was part Fen," Jon said. "Tell me about the dogs."

"There were two of them, and they walked side by side," Lin said. "They were so close I thought it was one animal with a lot of legs."

"Everything is scary out here," Jon said.

"I'm not scared!" Kyra's voice was defiant.

Lin put her hand over her brother's. "What route were you given?"

"To follow the twin Shan stars," Jon answered. "East of the Plain of Souls, across Gunda's Hope, then to the Swarm Mountains, Orenllag, and then the Ancient Land."

"We went out before the Fens had actually started the attack. We headed west of the Plain," Lin said. "But we ran into the Fens about four days out. There were five of us. I don't know what became of the others."

As she talked, Jon tried to remember whether he had seen her in Crystal City. He thought he might have spoken to her once when he discovered her playing a lute in one of the city's three gardens. She had been younger then, and the times more peaceful.

"You can travel with me," Jon said.

"We don't want to travel with you," Kyra said. "You're part Fen!"

Jon turned to face Kyra. He was almost as tall as Jon, but his face was rounder, his eyes set deeply beneath a high forehead.

"Whatever you want," Jon said. He wasn't going to defend his mother's having been part Fen, not out here in the Wilderness.

"I want to travel with you," Lin said. A swirl of dust rose up from the ground in front of them and spun skyward for a brief instant before seeming to fold in on itself and settle again to the earth. "We only have each other."

"Good." Jon touched Lin's shoulder lightly.

He started to walk again, and saw from the corner of his eye that both Lin and Kyra were following. He was glad.

They walked for hours, until Jon's knees ached with the effort. There were few places to walk in Crystal City; it was less than seven kilometers wide and most of it was taken up either with living spaces, centers where they grew the food they ate, the gardens, or the Societal Planning Centers. It was in the Planning Centers that they exercised three times a week. Okalians over fifteen, before the Fen attacks began, could go out of the City to hunt for new foods, or the occasional piece of fruit. Both men and women over eighteen went out once a week on safety patrols. It was on one of these patrols that they had first learned that the Fens were planning to attack them.

Jon slowed down when he thought they should rest. Lin and Kyra at first slowed down, then Kyra moved ahead.

"I thought we could stop here," Jon said, stopping in a field of coarse grass. "There's enough shelter and we can take turns sleeping."

"All right," Lin said.

She went a short distance from him and sat on the ground. Kyra turned back to her, but, instead of sitting, walked back and forth nervously.

Jon took his boots off and realized that the side of his ankle was sore. His feet and legs ached. He looked over at Lin. She saw him looking and turned away.

The night was relatively clear and he searched the sky for the twin stars. He found them and drew an arrow on the ground pointing

23

in the direction indicated by lining up the two stars. Far to the south, like a red eye burning over the brooding hills, was the Red Moon that hung over the Ancient Land.

"I think I've seen you at Crystal City," he called to Lin. "You were playing a lute. I said something to you."

"I don't remember you," Lin said. "But I know who your mother is. She's a small woman, almost fragile."

"Yes." Jon closed his eyes. An image of his mother, he had never thought of her as fragile, came to him. The fear he felt when he heard the sounds of the fighting, when he saw the changed looks on the faces of the adults, had entered him, had filled his chest like a vulture consuming him. Maybe it was just the way his body reacted, heart pounding, arms and legs trembling, mouth dry, that made him think so much of himself, to fear so much for himself. Now, in a moment of relative calm, he thought of his mother, and every feeling that had gathered in his chest rose into his throat and filled his eyes with tears. He rolled onto his stomach and put his face on the ground.

He woke with a start, opening his eyes to a sky shimmering with the first rays of sunlight. He didn't see or hear anything wrong, but he knew something had awakened him. Then there was a noise from somewhere ahead of him in the deep grass.

"Lin?" He looked around for Lin and her brother. He didn't see them.

The noise ahead of him sounded like something thrashing about through the grass. He imagined Fens. Pushing himself up slowly, he edged toward the sound. Then it stopped. Jon listened. He heard something that could have been heavy breathing.

In the middle of the clearing, standing in a shaft of morning light filtering softly through the low treetops, was a black unicorn. It was caught in a trap of thick vines, which bound its legs.

The unicorn's eyes rolled wildly as it twisted and turned trying to free itself. Its coat was shiny, and sweat foamed like pearl droplets on its powerful neck. The sun glinted off its black body as it reared back and twisted in a vain effort to free itself. Then it fell to one side and pawed at the vines with its feet. For a while it was still, and then it began to struggle again.

"What are we going to do?"

Lin's voice startled Jon and he jumped. She smiled at him and he smiled back.

"I don't know," he said. "Do you have any ideas?"

"When he moves, the vines tighten," she said.

"He needs help. We could free him if he lets us get close enough."

"Could be," Jon said. He looked around for a loose branch and found one. He picked it up and it broke in his hand. He looked over to where Lin, and now Kyra, watched.

Jon took a step toward the unicorn. The frightened animal twisted and tried to pull away from him.

"It's going to hurt itself," Lin said.

"Somebody set this trap," Jon said. "If we're going to free it, we'd better do it quickly!"

He went toward the unicorn again and it tried to wrench away from him.

"Remember the unicorns back in Crystal City?" Lin said. "If you approach them gently, they don't run away."

"If this one is from Crystal City it's probably been through as much we have," Jon said. "It's terrified, and we can't spend too much time here."

Jon looked for another branch, picked up several before he found one that didn't break, and poked it toward where the vine had been tied to a tree. The unicorn lunged at the branch, only to be pulled up sharply by the vines. It fell again. Lin ran to the tree and tried pulling at the vine.

"Kyra, help us!" Lin called to her brother. Jon

looked over at the boy, who shook his head and backed away.

Jon pushed the branch toward the unicorn to distract him as Lin struggled with the vine.

"Kyra!" Lin called to her brother again and this time he went flying toward her. He threw his weight against the vine, pulling with everything he had. One vine came loose but there was another one to deal with, too. Jon took a deep breath, and went quickly to the unicorn. He put his arms around the unicorn's neck and held on as tightly as he could.

The unicorn shook violently in his grasp, knocking Jon away. The animal lunged at Jon once and then turned toward Lin and Kyra.

"He's free!" Lin cried as she scrambled away.

The unicorn snorted, twisted, and leaped nearly straight into the air. Then, realizing it was free, it lowered its great head and raced off with long, powerful strides.

Jon, struggling to catch his breath, watched as the unicorn moved easily along the far edge of the field.

"It's so beautiful," Lin said. "But we'd better get out of here. If there are any Fens around, they had to have heard us."

They started out again, talking about the unicorn. Okalians didn't eat flesh, and the unicorns were the only animals in Crystal City.

They were largely kept in one of the gardens, but it wasn't unusual to see them wandering about the city.

They walked faster than they had the day before, and after a while Lin and Kyra dropped behind and walked together. They walked for hours, until they reached what looked like a sunken field. Its dusty surface was flecked with shiny chips of hard stone. They decided to go around it.

Along the edges of the field, barren trees pointed at odd angles toward the east. At the base of the trees was a green shrub.

"Berries," Lin said.

"They might be poisonous," Jon answered.

"No, look."

A tiny bird, black except for yellow markings on its wings, hopped near the shrub. It went from branch to branch pecking at the berries.

Lin watched the bird and then went to gather some of the berries herself. She brought the first handful to Kyra, who sat apart from them. She brought some to Jon.

"You said you ran into Fens?"

"When we saw them we panicked." Lin spoke softly. "Everything I had been taught just went out of my mind. We were all screaming . . . I was screaming. It was just horrible."

"Were many . . . injured?"

"I don't know. I can only remember it in bits and pieces," Lin said. "Does that make sense?"

"I think so," Jon answered.

"I remember us running. Screaming. Kyra fell and they grabbed him and were dragging him somewhere. That's how he was scratched up. He was kicking and swinging at them and I was yelling and trying to knock them off. Somehow we got free. He was like a wild person. He's been different ever since."

"He's young," Jon said.

"He's older now," Lin said. She had the juice of the berries on her face. "After the fighting was over, when Kyra and I had managed to get away, I didn't feel very much like I thought I should feel."

"Like an Okalian?" Jon asked.

Lin nodded.

Jon thought of saying that he didn't know if he felt the way an Okalian would feel, either. He didn't feel particularly brave, or noble, or strong.

"When we reach the Ancient Land it'll be different," Jon said. "We'll be real Okalians again."

"Yes. I believe that," Lin said. "I believe that with all my heart."

"It's following us!" Kyra called out suddenly.

Jon turned quickly to where Kyra knelt.

"I see it!" Lin said. "It's the unicorn we freed."

The unicorn stood off from them, motionless. Jon shielded his eyes from the bright haze and looked at it. It moved slowly ahead a few steps, stopped, and then retreated.

"Let's walk a bit," Lin said.

They started to walk and the unicorn started also.

"It's got to be one of the unicorns from Crystal City," Jon said. "And it's out here the same way we are, trying to find something safe in the Wilderness."

"It's beautiful." Lin shielded her eyes with her hand. "And so black it looks like a shadow against the sky," she said.

"I think it's good luck," Jon said.

"Fens believe in luck," Lin said. "We were taught that in school."

Jon took a deep breath and put his head down as he walked. Was that the reason that he did not feel like an Okalian? Because he was part Fen?

"It's still following us!" Kyra called out. He ran ahead of them, delighted to see the unicorn.

Lin caught up with Jon. "Jon, I think I believe in luck, too," she said. "I think we'll need a lot of it."

The wind, which earlier had come from the west, now came from the south into their faces as they walked. It was a strong wind, more humid than the one from the west, and heavier with dust. They talked less and rested more often.

"There's more new growth," Lin said to Jon as they came to a wide valley. "Look, there and there."

There was more green than he had been told to expect. Low shrubs dotted the floor of the valley and a few of the trees had leaves, but most were covered with a dull green growth around their trunks.

"You're in a good mood today," Jon said.

"She's always in a good mood," Kyra said. "She's the best sister in the world."

"And Kyra is the best brother," Lin said, putting her arm around him. "We both feel a little better about our chances. We haven't seen

32

any Fens since the bridge. Maybe they're all up at Crystal City."

"And our parents are beating them," Kyra said. "The Fens are going to be sorry that they attacked us."

"I think so," Jon said.

"It's simple. What we have to do," Lin went on, "is just to stay strong. It should take us twenty-four days at the most to reach the Ancient Land. We're all strong enough to do it. I know we are."

"We can get across this valley in no time," Kyra added.

"No, this is the Plain of Souls," Jon said. "Once we're in the middle of the Plain we can be seen from every side. That's what happened to the Okalians when they were on their way to start Crystal City. We'll be better off going east. Over there."

Jon pointed toward the rim of the valley.

"Going around will be harder," Lin said. "Maybe even a lot harder."

"Can you make it?" Jon asked.

"I have to make it," she answered.

Lin started walking and Kyra started after her. Jon let them get a short distance away from him before he started after them.

Lin was walking fast, faster than Jon thought she should. He had a funny feeling about how she looked. He thought about what she had said, about it being simple to reach the Ancient Land. His father had spoken like that, too. He had given Jon long lists of rules and things to look out for. Many of the things his father warned him about he already knew from school. Don't eat strange plants or fruits, don't let the dust that covered nearly everything stay on your skin for very long, and never underestimate the periods of cold. It was his mother who told him that there were more important things to think about. Like the way the sun felt on his skin, or the lingering taste of fresh fruit in his mouth.

He thought of a tune his mother often played on the orange lacquered lute she liked so much. He thought of her sitting in the soft glow of candlelight in the evenings, her fingers dancing across the strings of the instrument, a faraway look in her eyes.

"The lute is a happy instrument," she used to say. "Meant to be played by happy people. Or people who want to be happy."

Both of his parents had come to him the night before he left, when they first realized that Crystal City would fall to the Fens. His father had told him he depended on him to be strong. His mother had found a reason to stay behind, as she always did, and had told him to think not only of what he would be leaving, but of the love he would take with him as well.

Jon caught up with Lin.

"Kyra's walking really fast," he said. Kyra was up ahead, walking in long, loping strides, both arms stretched out to his sides.

"I think he needs to use up a lot of energy," Lin answered.

"He seems to be getting on all right," Jon said.

"Sometimes at night he cries," Lin said. "He doesn't want you to know it."

"It's all right to feel bad, even to cry."

"Your mother really doesn't look like the other Fens," Lin said, changing the subject.

Jon looked at her, and then away. "No, not really," he said. "She's taller, much taller. She's only part Fen. At any rate my father says that most Fens look the way they do because they have bad diets. If they ate better they would be like us . . . like the Okalians."

"Do you really believe that?" Lin asked.

"I don't know."

"Do you look like her?"

"Same hair, same eyes," Jon said. "Sometimes, when my father wasn't around, she would make me stand in front of the mirror with her and we would stand there looking at each other. She used to say 'Our souls come together in our eyes.'"

"I try not to think about my parents," Lin said. "Or about Crystal City."

"The thoughts keep coming, though," Jon continued. "They keep coming and it just hurts . . ."

"It just gets to the point where I feel the pain is part of me," Lin said. "The part that hurts so much. I can't talk about it, even with Kyra, without crying."

"It's the not knowing . . ." Jon started to say more, but Lin lifted her hand for him to stop, and he did.

They walked on without talking for a long while. There were things Jon thought about saying. He wondered what Lin's parents were like and what they had told Lin and Kyra. He also wondered what Lin really thought about the Okalians who were caught by the Fens.

Quickly he shut the thoughts away. He made himself think about his route and about the Book of Orenllag. The Okalians had made it from the Ancient Land as a people, across the difficult lands, through Gunda's Hope and the Plain of Souls, to reach a new beginning. He told himself that he and the other Okalian children would make a new beginning as well.

Kyra stopped first and sprawled on his belly. In the distance the unicorn loped easily. The boy was watching him.

"Kyra," Jon called. "Let's give him a name."

"I've got a name," Kyra called back.

"Not you," Lin said, "the unicorn."

"Let's call him Shadow!" Kyra said as Lin and Jon neared him.

"Then it'll be Shadow," Jon said. "Shall we touch hands or something?"

"Is that what Fens do?" Kyra asked.

"Jon is not a Fen," Lin said quietly. "He is an Okalian."

"We can touch hands if you want," Kyra said.

They stood, touched hands with Lin's on the top on her brother's and Jon's on the bottom. Jon lifted their hands slowly. "We have named him Shadow!" he said.

They found comfortable positions and rested. Jon closed his eyes and rolled his shoulders forward. It felt good.

"Shadow's leaving," Kyra called.

They sat up. The unicorn they had just named was off to their right. They watched as the dark shape moved easily across the field, silhouetted against the flat gray-white sky. Shadow was a perfect name for him.

"Kyra! Over there! Can you see them?" There was panic in Lin's voice.

"What is it?" Jon asked.

"There!" She pointed straight ahead. "That's why Shadow is leaving. It's the dogs!"

Jon didn't see anything that looked like dogs in the direction Lin was looking, only a vague gray mass that seemed to move of its own accord. Looking closer, he saw that the mass was really a pack of living creatures, one jammed against the other, pushing and jostling one another as they made their way toward them.

"Into the trees," Jon said.

They moved quickly and without speaking. They found a tree they thought they could climb and stood near it. Then they turned back to the dogs.

The beasts seemed to be wandering aimlessly, their heads close to the ground. Their howls were like the whistling of a distant wind, cold and eerie.

"They're the same kind I saw before," Lin said. "We didn't learn anything about them from the Council. Did you?"

"No," Jon answered. "What were they doing before?"

"The same as now," she said. "Just moving together like that."

The dogs on the outside of the pack kept going in toward the center, pushing their way into the middle of the others, forcing other dogs to the outside. They went along at a slow pace.

"Look, they've stopped," Lin said.

They had. They were yelping now, and most of them sat or lay down. Two of them circled the pack. They went around and around. The pitch of the yelping got higher. Then, suddenly, they started again.

"Into the tree! Quickly!" Jon said.

Jon started to give Lin a hand up. The tree was rock hard.

"It's dead!" Lin called out. "The limbs might break off!"

The dogs were getting nearer, picking up speed. "We don't have a choice!" he said.

He pushed Lin up as far as he could until she reached the bottom branch. She pulled herself up slowly. She went up into the tree until she reached a thicker branch and stopped there. Kyra was up next, stepping roughly on Jon's shoulder. The yelping of the dogs increased.

"Jon, hurry!" Lin's voice was filled with urgency.

Jon had to wait until Kyra had cleared the bottom branches. The dogs were coming faster, yelping and growling. He watched as Kyra got into the higher branches.

"Kyra, be careful!" Lin called down. "Stay near the trunk!"

"I'm being careful," Kyra said. He was watching the dogs as he climbed.

"Hurry! Hurry!" Lin's voice pleaded, and Jon

pulled himself up just as the dogs reached them.

The lowest branch seemed weak, but it had taken all of Jon's strength to reach it. The dogs raced past the tree, and on to a small mound beyond it.

Bigger than they seemed from a distance, most were gray and only a few black.

"They're stopping," Kyra said. His voice was calm, calmer than it should have been.

The dogs were settling on the hill. Two dogs broke loose from the pack and began to circle it, their noses close to the ground. The yelping of the dogs circling the pack changed, as if they were signaling the others. The pack shifted slowly, took up the yelping, and headed back toward the trees.

This time they came slowly, jostling and pushing against each other, until they came to the tree where Jon, Lin, and Kyra waited. One dog moved heavily into the trunk. He sniffed at its base and then put his paws on the trunk and began to yelp. Jon carefully moved to the next branch. The dog was close enough for Jon to see why they moved in a pack, and so strangely. He looked down at the snarling mouth and the white, sightless eyes, and trembled.

A aack!" Kyra made a noise and started spitting at the dogs.

"Shut up!" Jon yelled at him.

The dogs kept up their snarling and yelping for a while and then moved a short distance away, piling onto one another. At first the pile was loose, but it got tighter and tighter as the dogs settled in.

"Hang on!" Jon called out. "We have to stay strong."

"You're scared!" Kyra called out.

"Yes, I'm scared."

"I'm not!" he called back.

At the sound of their voices, the dogs rose and began yelping and growling. They headed for the tree, some stopping a few meters away and baring their teeth.

Jon looked up at Kyra. He was clinging with both arms to the tree. He was scared. Not as scared as Jon was, perhaps, but still scared.

One dog came up to the tree and barked. He lifted his head, baring a row of vicious-looking teeth. He went around the tree several times, and then went back over to the pile of dogs and pushed his way into them.

They kept as quiet as possible. Jon was scared, but he was angry and frustrated, too. He had left Crystal City with the other children, running from the invasion of the Fens. Now he was cold, and terrified of the dogs. Was this to be his life, running from everything? Struggling just to survive?

"Shadow!" Lin broke the silence.

A dog, hearing Lin's voice, yelped and ran around the base of the tree. He was answered by other dogs.

Jon saw Shadow. The unicorn stood on a small crest near the edge of the valley. Jon knew that even with his great strength he would be no match for the dogs. There were too many of them.

It began to snow. It swirled about the tree as the wind picked up.

Both Lin and Kyra stretched out their bodies on branches above him while Jon sat with his legs over a smaller branch, his arms around the trunk of the tree. The snow went down the back of his neck and he began to shiver. His fingers ached from the cold and from time to time his foot would go to sleep. Below him, huddled against the swirling snow, were the dogs. In the distance, the movement of shadows and lights were nightmare dancers that called to him, their voices through the dead branches inviting him to release his grip from the tree.

Jon fought the sleep that tugged at him. Each breath became painful as the cold air froze the moisture inside his nostrils.

He could see Kyra plainly; one of the boy's feet dangled from a branch just above him. He was turning his face, trying to avoid the stinging snow. Jon looked for Lin but wasn't sure the dark spot above him was she. He looked down to the ground, but he didn't see her there, either.

"Lin!" He called to her.

"I'm still here!" The answer came from high above him. Lin had climbed farther into the tree.

"Is Kyra awake?"

"Yes!" the boy answered. "There are Fens coming!"

Everything on Jon's body hurt. He looked down at the dogs. They were moving again, going about in quick circles, searching for a scent. Then Jon smelled what the dogs had — the strong odor of smoke.

"Where are the Fens?" Jon called out. "Are they headed this way?"

"They're on the far side of the valley," Lin said. "I don't know if they're really Fens, and I can't tell if they're coming this way. They're carrying torches."

Jon strained to see through the snow, but couldn't. Below him the dogs circled about the tree and yelped. Some howled. The circle grew wider. One dog started off, then two others followed it. They caught up with it and the yelping began again as they huddled away from the others. The others followed, bumping and jostling each other until they were all assembled. They started off in a quick pace away from the odor of the smoke. They moved fast and were soon nearly invisible in the falling snow.

"The torches are headed in this direction," Lin said.

When it was clear that the dogs were gone, Jon slid down to the ground. Kyra came down and then Lin. Halfway down the trunk of the tree she pushed away from it and jumped. She landed on her feet but her legs gave way and she fell to the ground.

Lin winced. Her hair fell across her face and she pushed it away in anger.

"Why do we have to be out here?" she cried. "Why?"

Kyra knelt by her side as she gritted her teeth.

"We have to go on," Jon said.

Lin looked up at him, her eyes filled with tears, and tightened the corners of her mouth. She pulled herself to her feet, wincing as she did.

Jon could see the faint lights from the torches. They weren't that near.

"Those Fens will tear up the dogs," Kyra said, seeing Jon look toward them.

"I don't know," Jon answered. "If the dogs aren't afraid of the fire, it will be children with sticks against wild dogs. I don't know —"

"They're not children!" Lin's voice was filled with anger. "They're not children! *We* are children. They are Fens!"

"Most of them are younger than I am," Jon said. "Some people on the Council think the plague might be over, but they still don't live that long."

"I don't care how long they live!" Lin said. "It's because of them that we're out here. We're children and children shouldn't be out in the cold and running from dogs and climbing into trees and . . . and being away from our parents.

They aren't children. Children don't attack Okalians!"

"We have to go on," Jon said quietly.

He walked ahead of them, letting his feet drag so that he broke a path through the fallen snow.

He was cold. He had almost forgotten that he was cold, or how cold he was. As he walked he thought about what Lin had said, that the Fens weren't children. He wondered what the Fens thought of them.

t was during the time of Gunda that the Okalians were forced to leave the Ancient Land," Jon said, as much to hear the sound of his own voice as anything else. "The dust was thicker over the Ancient Land so that they couldn't even see the moon. It was just a dark shape in the sky."

"I know that," Lin said. "You don't have to give me history lessons."

"Did you know that it was on the Plain of Souls that more Okalians had their dreaming stopped than at any other place on the journey?" Jon went on.

"Yes, I've read the Book of Orenllag," Lin answered sharply. "The same as you. But it didn't tell us about the Fens."

"The Elders who wrote the Book of Orenllag didn't know the Fens would ever attack us," Jon said.

"Attack us?" Lin glared at Jon. "The Fens *kill*

people. In Crystal City the Okalians dream until they have grown old and their dreaming stops, or some . . . some terrible chance has fallen on us. But the Fens *kill*! They kill animals to eat. They kill Okalians. That's what makes them different from us. They kill!"

"I know that," Jon said. He turned sharply on his heel and walked away from Lin. He could feel the hurt and anger rising in his chest, his face burning. He was part Fen. Perhaps it was not a large part, but still it was true.

He walked as fast as he could, hoping that Lin and Kyra wouldn't keep up with him. He knew his route. He would follow the twin Shan stars, stay east of the Plain of Souls, cross Gunda's Hope, and go past the Swarm Mountains on to Orenllag. From there he would be able to see the Ancient Land. He didn't need to be with anyone. He could be with himself.

Off to his right there was a noise. It sounded far away. Jon couldn't think of what the sound was; he almost didn't care. He thought of his mother, half Okalian, half Fen. He had never met his Fen grandmother. It didn't matter. Nothing mattered except that he was strong, and that he would find the Ancient Land.

"Jon, I'm sorry." Lin was breathless as she caught up to him. "I forgot that you were part Fen."

"It doesn't matter," he answered.

"It matters," Lin said. "I don't want to hurt you. I want us to be together."

Jon stopped. He looked at Lin to see if she was sincere. She looked at him, pleading with her eyes for him to put aside his anger.

"So it matters," Jon said. "I know what the Fens have done, and I hate it as much as you do. But we are Okalians, you and I, and I know that you took the same vow as I did, to find the Ancient Land and —"

"— and a new beginning," Lin finished the oath they had all taken.

Jon began walking again, this time more slowly, with Lin at his side.

They pushed on for hours, half looking for a place to stop and rest, half afraid to stop. When they finally did stop it was near a small frozen stream that ran between the Plain of Souls and a rocky ridge. There were small animals on the ridge with lizard tails and horned backs. They darted along the ridge, stopping abruptly to some unseen signal, only to mysteriously resume their frantic flights along the hard earth to disappear in the darkness or beneath the snow.

"We can take turns sleeping," Jon said.

"I know that," Lin said. "We're equals here, you're not our leader."

"I didn't say I was," Jon said. "It's just that the thought of sleeping sounds so good to me. Closing my eyes even for a moment is like something so good I want to eat it."

"Then close your eyes," Lin said. "You sleep first, and then we'll wake you and we'll sleep."

Jon lay on his stomach and closed his eyes. He called sleep, welcomed it, tried to suck it into his lungs, into his belly. But sleep didn't come. Instead came the thoughts that he had been pushing aside for so long. What had happened at the city? He imagined what he had not wanted to imagine, the Fens breaking through the outer walls, running through the halls of Crystal City, stopping the dreaming . . . killing the Okalians.

He thought of Veton, his father. His father would be brave and resourceful, not like him, scared. He squeezed his eyes tightly shut and tried desperately to block out the images that tumbled into his mind. They were images of his mother. Of her standing in the halls, her gentle hands before her, the hands that had caressed her lute, and her son. He imagined her looking at them, wondering what she should do with them as the Fen children came toward her . . .

When Kyra woke him, he saw he was lying on the ground near Lin's feet. He raised himself to his elbow.

51

"What's wrong?"

"Nothing is wrong. The unicorn is back," Kyra said. There were dark marks on his face — stripes on his forehead and smudged diagonals under his eyes.

"What's that on your face?" Jon asked.

"Nothing," Kyra answered.

Jon had seen markings on the faces of the Fens. Kyra didn't look like a Fen, but he didn't look like himself, either.

They were on a small hill and Shadow was standing at the bottom of it. Jon wondered if the unicorn thought they would lead him back to Crystal City.

"Their gentleness and elegance," his father had said, "symbolizes our way of life better than any other creature or thing."

When Lin was fully awake, Jon told her to look at her brother.

"Why?" she asked.

"Just look at him," Jon said.

Jon watched as Lin went to her brother. She at first frowned and looked away, and then took Kyra's face in her hands. She touched his face and tried to wipe the markings off, but he wouldn't let her. Lin moved away from him, but she was clearly shaken. Kyra walked ahead of them, sometimes moving straight ahead, sometimes hurrying to a tree or bush where he would stand for a moment, as if he were stalking something, before moving on.

"Is he okay?"

"He's fine," Lin said.

"Why did he mark his face up?"

"I don't know," Lin said, her words spoken so softly Jon could hardly hear her. "He'll be all right."

There had been a time when Jon thought that the Okalians understood most things. Now, even as an Okalian, he saw that there were things he didn't understand. Kyra was one of those things.

Jon wasn't at all sure that Kyra would be all right, or even strong enough to make the journey to the Ancient Land, but he didn't say that to Lin.

Most of the Plain of Souls had been barren and sandy. There were patches of short, matted grass and occasionally a shrub with tiny white flowers. As they went farther south, the grass was thicker and there were trees with thick, twisted branches.

Jon saw a bug crawling in the undergrowth. It was bright red with yellow spots and had red and yellow spikes on its body. Jon had never seen one like it before. For Jon it was as if there were a whole new order of life, things that had come into being only after he had left Crystal City.

"Jon, over there!" Lin whispered hoarsely.

Jon looked quickly toward where Lin was pointing. Squinting, he saw a crudely built fence that closed off a circular area. In front of the fence a kneeling figure was digging with a stick.

Jon motioned for them to get down. Behind them Shadow pawed anxiously at the ground.

Lin crawled to Jon. "What is it?" she asked. "Some kind of fort?"

"I don't know," Jon answered. "I think we'd better stay clear of it."

"It's a boy," Lin said. "He's standing!"

Jon looked and saw a tall, thin young man. He was looking intently at something cradled in his hands. He started away, then went back to where he had been digging. He knelt and started digging again with the stick.

"I think he's an Okalian," Jon said.

They watched him a while longer and Jon realized that he was glad just to find another Okalian.

"Are you sure?" Lin asked.

"No."

Just then the figure straightened up again and

looked out toward them. He dropped what he had been digging and shielded his eyes as he looked around. Behind him Jon saw a thin wisp of smoke rise slowly and then flatten out in the heavy air.

"He's an Okalian," Lin said, standing. She waved to him, and he waved both arms over his head.

Jon glanced over toward Kyra. The boy was kneeling, his hands clutched in front of him. He was afraid. Jon couldn't blame him; Kyra had been captured once. Jon turned his attention back to the fence.

Jon stood and they started toward the fence. As they drew near it was clear that the figure was an Okalian. He wore a metal band around the upper part of his right arm, as some older Okalians did.

"Hello, friends!" His voice was cheery enough.

"Hello!" Lin responded.

"Come in, come in," he said, motioning toward an opening in the fence. "I thought you looked like Okalians."

"How long have you been here?" Jon asked, stopping in front of the crudely made door.

"Awhile," he said. "But come on in. You can't be too careful, you know."

Jon felt uncomfortable going into the opening. The boy's clothing was dirty and torn, and he seemed strange. Near the door he stood to one side, nervously rubbing his thin arms.

"Two? Three of you! That's good. Are there more?"

"Us, and Shadow," Jon said, looking around for the unicorn. He saw him and walked toward him, only to see the animal move quickly away.

"He'll come later," Jon said. "He follows us."

"A unicorn? Wonderful. It's been a long time since I've seen a unicorn."

"My name is Jon."

"And I am Ceb," he said. "We call this place the Compound, for want of a better name."

"What route are you following?" Lin asked.

"This is my home," Ceb said. "You're welcome to be here. What are your names?"

"I am Lin." She stepped forward. "This is my brother Kyra. How long have you been here?"

"We were wandering along the edge of the Plain," Ceb went on, "like you. Then we came upon this place. It must have been built ages ago."

"There are others here?" Jon asked.

"You'll meet them," Ceb said. "Do you want water?"

"Yes," Jon heard himself say quickly.

Ceb smiled. "We have fresh water," he said. "Come."

They had moved away from the opening in the fence and Jon saw that Shadow had come into the Compound. It made him feel somehow more secure.

From the inside the fence looked stronger than it did from the outside. There was a heavy bolt that could be placed across the gate that would keep out animals, but the fence was too low to keep out Fens.

Inside the Compound was a large structure surrounded by smaller ones. The smaller ones were little more than huts made of stone and mud. Jon saw faces in the doorways, sometimes just parts of faces, eyes peering from the shadows. The large structure, the one that Ceb led them into, was made of branches woven together and sealed with a dark material.

Jon saw Lin looking around in the dim light with the same wonder he had.

"You said you've been here for a while," Lin told Ceb. "Why do you stay?"

"We stay because we are happy here," Ceb said. He smiled in a strange, almost pained, manner. "We weren't in the city when the Fens attacked."

Shadow whinnied and stamped his foot.

"For a while we wandered around like I imagine you're doing," Ceb went on. "Being afraid of everything, and for every moment of our lives. Then we found this place and stopped to rest."

"You're going to stay here?" Lin asked.

"Until it's time to leave," Ceb answered quickly. "Are you a family?"

"Yes," Lin answered before Jon had even thought about what Ceb meant.

"Then I'll try to find you a place together," Ceb said. He smiled broadly before leaving.

"What is this place about?" Lin wondered aloud when Ceb had disappeared through the low door.

"I think we're being watched," Jon said. "Did you see them?"

Lin nodded.

"We'll have to be careful," Jon said.

Presently Ceb came back. There were two Okalian girls with him and a boy no older than Kyra. The girls seemed to be nearly as old as Ceb. They carried gourds of water.

"What do you think?" Lin whispered in Jon's ear.

"I don't know," he answered under his breath.

"This is Atalia and her sister Pan," Ceb introduced the two girls. "And this is Atun. They've agreed to share their space with you. We don't have that much room here, so we do the best we can."

Ceb nodded and left them with the girls and boy.

Lin drank hungrily from one of the gourds. The water ran down her face and onto her tunic. Kyra drank next, and then Jon.

"Come with us," the darker girl said.

"How many of you are here?" Lin asked, as they followed them.

"Twelve of us," Atalia said, glancing back at Jon.

The inside of the tiny hut looked like a cave. It was clean and neat, though, and away from danger. The soup they were given was warm and delicious, and Jon felt himself relax. The girls began to talk, to ask how things had gone at Crystal City.

"Not well," Lin answered. "We don't know the final outcome . . . but it didn't look good."

"Let's not talk about it," Pan said.

"How old is Ceb?" Jon asked.

"Eighteen," Pan said. "He knows a lot."

Jon felt that the Compound was wrong and the Okalians who lived there, who did not want to make the journey to the Ancient Land, were somehow wrong, too.

They drank more of the cool water, and then

were given places to rest. Jon wanted to think about the Compound, to figure it out, but in minutes he was asleep.

When he finally woke it was to the sound of girls' voices.

"Look who's with us again!"

Jon looked up and saw Atalia. She was wrapped in a white cloth and her hair was loosened about her shoulders.

"Have I slept long?" he asked.

"Forever," Lin said from the other side of the small hut.

"How are you doing?" he asked.

"Well enough to start traveling soon," she said. There was a seriousness in her eyes as she looked at him. The corners of her mouth moved slightly, as if there was something more she wanted to say, that simply wouldn't come.

"There's no hurry," Atalia said. She spoke quickly. "We're glad to have you here."

"Don't you want to get to the Ancient Land?" Jon asked her.

"Maybe." Atalia giggled. "And maybe not."

In the dim light Atalia's teeth looked dark.

"How do you spend your time here?"

"Sometimes we tell stories." Atalia was preparing food. "We have the Book of Orenllag. Sometimes we read to one another, or just rest."

"We visit each other a lot," Pan said. "Come on, I'll show you around."

She took Jon's hand and pulled him up. He looked around. He didn't see Kyra.

With Pan holding his hand, he left the small hut and went out into the courtyard. It was nearly dark and he closed his eyes to get used to it. When he opened them again, his whole body tensed and he stepped back quickly, bumping into Pan and nearly falling.

"Don't be afraid!" Pan said quickly. "They won't harm you."

"What are they doing here?" He stared straight ahead at three Fens. They stood together in the center of the inner court of the Compound.

"We live in peace here," Pan said. "We've learned to do that."

"You learned that from Ceb?"

She didn't answer.

The Fens, with their peculiar, waddling gait, started toward them. Pan, who was slightly taller than the Fens, stepped forward and touched her fingertips together in front of her face. The Fens did the same thing. Then they smiled, or at least Jon imagined that what they were doing was smiling. Their eyes narrowed to slits and their lips moved away from their red-stained teeth.

"It means that all of our thoughts are of peace," Pan said.

"I think I'll check on Lin," Jon said.

When he got back to the hut he had slept in, Lin was waiting for him. She searched his face, trying to read his reaction. Kyra was there, too, sitting in the shadows. His arms were folded in front of him as he rocked back and forth. Jon wondered what was going on in the boy's mind. He knew that both Kyra and Lin had seen the Fens who lived in the Compound.

"Okalians have the mind to understand things," Atalia said, without asking if he had seen the Fens. "When you understand the ways of peace everything will be all right."

"We've taken an oath . . . ." Jon heard his voice tremble. "We've taken an oath to reach the Ancient Land."

"Of course," Atalia said, smiling. "Have some soup. Rest. There is so much in your head now. Later things will be easier."

Atalia ladled out the soup. She gave some to Lin, and then to Jon. She offered it to Kyra. He didn't look at her, just kept rocking to and fro. She put it in front of him.

He didn't touch it.

Jon tasted the soup. It was warm, and filling. He looked over at Lin. She was watching her brother.

"There were nearly white clouds in the sky last week." Pan spoke to Atalia. "Did Ceb tell you?"

"Yes, it means there might be clear rain soon," Atalia said.

"When I was young I used to imagine myself riding on a white cloud and going to a secret place that only I would know about." Pan went on as if Jon and Lin and Kyra weren't there, as if they hadn't seen the Fens and weren't filled with wonder and fear that these creatures would attack them.

"Ridiculous," Atalia answered. "Because I know all the secret places that have ever been."

They laughed. They talked more, almost without stopping. They would go from one thing to the next almost without reason. They talked of Ceb a great deal, and it was clear that he was their leader.

Atun, the boy, wandered in and out of the hut, usually without speaking. Sometimes Jon would catch the young boy looking at him, only to see him look quickly away when their eyes met.

"Atun must tell a story," Pan said, noticing that Jon was looking at the boy. "He tells wonderful stories."

"I-I can't," Atun stammered.

Pan first, and then Atalia, went to him, and

they put their arms around him and their faces against his chest. Huddled that way, they even looked like Fens.

"Then you must have some sorpos," Pan said to Atun. She spoke to him, but she looked at Jon.

"All right," the boy said.

She went to a corner and reached into a basket, and took out a piece of reddish fruit. Atun took a bite from it while it was still in her hands. Then she gave it to Atalia.

Jon watched as Atalia bit greedily into the fruit. There was no control in the way the Okalian girl stuffed the fruit into her mouth. It was a hunger, a hunger that Jon had never seen before.

The sorpos was half as large as Pan's face, with a bright red and yellow peel. Inside it was dark red and shiny with juice. Atun greedily took more of it from Pan. The moment he had taken as much of it as he wanted, he turned and walked away. Without saying a word, he leaned against the wall and slid down until he was seated. His face was in shadow while a triangle of light fell across his thin legs. Atalia took several bites of the sorpos, ran the back of her hand across her mouth, and went to another corner and took a small ball from a nearby table. She sat cross-legged on the floor and began to play with the ball slowly, rolling it from one hand to the other.

Pan was standing in the middle of the room as the rest of the group watched. Her head was down and she was eating the sorpos. Then she lifted her head slowly and held out what was left of the fruit.

"Do you want sorpos?" she asked. She was smiling.

Lin turned away and went to the mat she had slept upon the night before. Pan, still smiling, offered it to Kyra.

"It doesn't bite, you know," she said.

Kyra took a small bite of the sorpos. He turned the fruit so he would not have to bite where Atun had. Pan went to Jon next and offered him some.

"What is it?"

"It gives you a nice feeling," she said. "I think it's one of those things between fruit and flesh."

"You know I don't eat flesh," Jon said, turning his head to avoid the sorpos.

"Of course not," she exhaled impatiently as if Jon had said something stupid. "I just mean it feels that way. I'm Okalian, after all."

Pan moved it near his mouth and then, stepping nearer, rubbed it gently across his lips. Jon moved his head back and pressed his lips together.

"It feels prickly," Pan said with a low giggle, and Jon bit into it.

"It does taste like fruit, but different," Jon said as he rubbed his mouth.

Kyra said he wanted more, but Pan wouldn't allow it. "Later, perhaps," she said.

She finished the rest of it herself while Kyra went over to where Lin was lying on a mat near the wall. Lin looked tired. Her breathing was shallow and her shoulders drooped. Kyra sat next to her and she put her head in his lap, but it was he who went to sleep first, with Lin following shortly. Soon Atalia and Atun were also asleep.

"What did you do in the Crystal City?" Jon asked Pan, who was still awake.

"I was going to be a teacher," she said. "I would have liked that, I think. Sometimes I try to teach Atun, but he doesn't want to listen. What were you going to do when you grew up?"

"I don't know," Jon answered. "My father thought I could be a scientist. My mother said maybe by the time I grew up we would have musicians again."

"You like music?"

"Yes, a lot," Jon answered. He felt as if he were going to sleep. He wasn't tired, but he knew something was happening. The small spot of sunlight on the floor before them had spread slowly. Jon felt it sucking him into its warmth, making him drowsy. Pan's voice continued. She was talking about water, how wonderful it was, and how she had felt once when she had waded in a stream in the Crystal City.

"It was as if I were flowing with the water," she said, "as if I were lighter than the air about me. I felt like one of those small things that spin webs and hang from trees, except that I wouldn't change into anything, just blow forever in the wind."

"That was good," Jon said, as he tried to stay awake.

"When I came here I was depressed," she said. "I thought I would never see real water again. Not the kind you can bathe in or swim in."

"There's none here," Jon said.

"No, but it doesn't matter," she said.

She came and sat next to Jon. Her eyes looked as if she might be crying, but when he leaned toward her and looked closer he could see that she wasn't. She leaned toward him, imitating what he was doing, and laughed. Her laugh was deep and pleasant.

"Where do you get the sorpos?" he asked.

"The Fens collect it. They leave at night and bring it back. They know where to get everything. They have sorpos and herbs that heal sickness. They're our ages, even younger, but they act older. You know what I mean?"

Jon's eyes had closed and he was not sure if he was awake or asleep. He had just suddenly slowed down. When he forced open his eyes, the top of Pan's head was in front of him and he saw that she was leaning toward him. He touched her hair. It was soft. He slept.

It was not exactly a dream, and not exactly wakefulness. He was somehow aware of the familiar things of his home back in Crystal City, the warmth, the comfort of knowing he could open his eyes and see his mother there as she had been so many times, sitting at the great carved table with her spinning. Perhaps it was half memory and half dream.

When he had awakened from his semi-dream he saw that Pan was sitting at the entrance of the sleeping place, talking with Atalia. She had a way of looking at Jon, a way that he liked, sliding her eyes toward him without moving her head.

"Peace to you!" Pan touched her breast over her heart and then held her open palm toward him.

"Peace to you!" Atalia said. She made the same gesture Pan had.

"Peace to you, too," Jon said, touching his chest quickly and holding his hand up.

"When someone offers you a greeting of peace you must return it," Pan said. "Peace is the secret of what we are about here."

"We're not Okalians, or Fens, but brothers

and sisters in peace," Atalia said. "There's fresh fruit here, and water outside in the center."

The already dim space darkened as a Fen stood for a moment in the doorway. Then she came in and Atalia and Pan started talking to her. It wasn't as if they were talking to a friend. It was as if they were talking to an honored guest, some person of esteem, a Council elder.

Jon stared at the Fen, straining to recognize something familiar, something of his mother. He remembered how his father would wonder aloud why she insisted upon claiming the strain of Fen blood that she had. Jon used to think that it was a charming thing, a sweet and gentle accent that made her just a little different, a little more special. This Fen girl seemed neither charming nor gentle. She was wearing an Okalian tunic over her shoulders, and her bare arms looked strong. She looked at Jon intently, almost defying him to return her gaze.

Jon took a deep breath, got up, and went out of the sleeping space. He felt good walking about the courtyard of the Compound. Mostly it was because of the warmth. The howling wind and the gelid air were beyond the fence of the Compound. Even if it got colder, he felt they could survive in the Compound.

There were more Fens. Jon tried to avoid their eyes as he looked about the Compound.

"Gebus!" Two of them spoke the word clearly as they stopped in front of him.

Jon stopped and looked down at the ground.

"Gebus!" One of them touched his chest and held an open hand toward Jon.

"Gebus," Jon said softly.

"They use the same word for peace, birth, and friendship." Ceb came up and laid a hand on Jon's shoulder. "They're being friendly."

There was a water bag in the middle of the Compound from which everyone drank. Jon poured some water into a gourd that was tied to the side of the bag. It was incredibly cold and good. Another Fen, his teeth almost glowing red from the sorpos, his eyes distant, came to the water bag and drank a little and poured the rest over his head. Then he walked away. Jon drank more, letting the cold water pour down his throat until it ached. It ran down the sides of his face and onto his neck and chest until he shivered with the delight of it.

"Lin is sick."

Jon turned to see Kyra standing next to him. "She's tired," he said.

"She'll be all right," Kyra answered, looking at Jon as if he expected he would answer some question he had not asked. "Pan said so."

Jon went back to the sleeping space and Ceb

was there. He was sitting with Pan and Atalia. There was a Fen sitting with them as well.

"Are there any medicines here?" he asked Ceb.

The Fen spoke to Jon. He thought he recognized some words in the language of the Okalians, but he wasn't sure.

He looked at Ceb.

"He understood you," Ceb said. "But the Fen people who live here don't always have the healing herbs. If they have them, they wear them in pouches about their necks."

"Do they really work?"

"For most things," Ceb said. "But the sorpos will help her as well. She hasn't taken any of it."

He put the sorpos down in front of Jon. "It will help her," he said.

Jon picked up the sorpos and took it to Lin. He touched her shoulder and she turned to him and tried to smile. He offered her the sorpos.

"I don't know if I want it," she said.

"They think it might help with your illness."

Jon started to move away but she caught his arm. She pulled herself up to one elbow and bit into the sorpos. Then she turned away again.

Jon told himself that the sorpos would help Lin. He was tired, and a feeling of sadness made it even worse. He lifted the sorpos to his lips. When he reached the mat he had slept on earlier, he stretched out on it.

For a long time he lay with his eyes closed, halfway between sleep and wakefulness. There was the sense that he wasn't really there. He lifted his hand to see if he could feel his face. He did, but it was an uneasy feeling. He felt suddenly afraid.

Opening his eyes, he pushed himself up from the floor and the world spun around violently. There was a lamp with a bright yellow flame on a hook on the wall. He lifted it and looked about as the reeling slowed. He could see the bodies of Pan and Atalia, Atun, and Ceb lying about the floor. They were all asleep. Jon crawled over to Lin and touched her head. It was cool and damp.

There was a noise from Ceb as he shifted position unconsciously. Jon looked and saw that Ceb had rolled onto his back. His eyes were only half closed and his mouth was wide open. A small insect settled on his face, walking near the red-stained mouth.

Jon crawled out of the sleeping space and into the darkness of the Compound.

The Fens were in the Compound. They had formed a line and were carrying something over their heads. He wanted to know what they were doing and hoped his legs were steady enough to follow them. Jon licked his dry lips and swallowed hard as he made his way along the wall to where Shadow had been earlier.

When Jon found Shadow trembling, he took off his tunic and put it over the unicorn's neck.

"It's all right, Shadow," he said. "It's all right."

He looked to see if Shadow had been injured but saw nothing. Jon put his arm around the animal's neck and turned his attention again to see what the Fens were doing.

It wasn't clear. He knew they were carrying something, something they had on a kind of platform above their heads. Two Fens with torches walked before it and two followed. They went across the center of the Compound to the entrance. One of them opened it and they carried the platform out. Moments later they returned. The entrance to the Compound was again closed and the heavy bolt that secured it put in place.

One by one, the torches went out until there was only one lit. This was held by a Fen who went to the gate and put his ear to it. Then he walked away. Jon watched in the darkness. The sorpos had left him feeling unsure of himself. He thought about going back to the sleeping space and looking for more of the red and yellow fruit, then decided not to.

Jon was about to go back to the hut when he saw the Fen with the torch go back to the gate and put his ear to it again. After a short while he waddled away.

As quietly as he could, Jon started making his way toward the gate. Reaching it quickly, he put his ear against it as the Fen had. He heard nothing.

The Fens had gone just outside the gate. Whatever it was they had carried, they had left there. Jon's hand went to the large bolt and pulled it back.

As the gate to the Compound closed behind him, he realized how scared he was. He didn't want to be out of the Compound, but he had to know what the Fens were doing. He stood near the gate for a while. It seemed to have grown colder. The New Moon shone on the gently falling snow. He listened but didn't hear anything. Now and again, between the slow, almost hypnotic patterns of the falling snow, he could see the twin Shan stars in the east.

He looked around, found the Fen footprints in the snow, and followed them with his eyes. They didn't go far, no more than twenty meters. There was something there, something still. He pushed one foot in front of him and then the other. He was afraid to look ahead and afraid not to. Finally, he reached a point near the still object and took a closer look at it.

There, face down, the piling snow already partially covering the shaggy skins over its body, was a Fen whose dreaming had stopped. He was still on the small platform on which the others had carried him out of the Compound. He had somehow stopped dreaming, and they had taken his body and put it away from them outside the fence.

Jon turned him over and looked closely. The Fen seemed older than the others, but not much. He looked at his mouth, now gaping open as if he were in a state of surprise, and saw the red stains of the sorpos.

He was about to start back toward the Compound when he heard a strange noise. At first he turned to the Fen, thinking it had come from him. The body didn't appear to have moved. Jon listened for a while, watching the Fen's mouth to see if he saw signs of breath.

The sound again. It was low, menacing. Then there was a yelp. The dogs!

Jon looked about frantically. He didn't see them but knew they were out there, among the shadows. It was what the Fen had been listening for.

Backing toward the gate, Jon saw a shadow move across the snow in front of him, then another. There was another yelp, and then a low growl. Now he saw the pack, jostling one another, pushing together as they scented their prey.

He touched the fence of the Compound and felt for the gate, opening it just as the pack surrounded the still figure on the platform.

The bolt was clumsy, and with his stiff fingers he had trouble moving it, but finally he managed it. Putting his ear to the door he heard the whining, growling dogs as they devoured their prey.

Ceb was spread-legged in the sleeping space. With his mouth open he looked like the Fen outside the Compound. His chest moved, though, and Jon knew he was still dreaming. He looked at the others. Pan and Atalia were sleeping next to the Fen girl they had been speaking to earlier. Kyra was by himself in a corner and Lin was next to the far wall. Jon went to her side and touched her face lightly with his fingertips.

Her eyes opened quickly and she looked at him. For a moment she didn't seem to recognize him, and then she smiled.

"Is it day?" she asked.

"Not yet," Jon answered. "How are you feeling?"

"Good," she answered. "It's warm here. Is Kyra asleep?"

"By himself in a corner," Jon said.

"Are you all right?"

"Yes," he said. He didn't want to worry her. "I was outside the Compound for a while. I saw the Fens taking something outside and leaving it. I wondered what it was and I went to look."

"What was it?" she asked.

"The body of a Fen," he said. "His dreaming had stopped. They took the body out and left it for the dogs."

"I don't think the dogs would be in this area," she said.

"Perhaps not," he said. He didn't tell her that he had *seen* the dogs, or that a Fen had listened for them at the Compound gate. He didn't know what to make of it and decided to ask Ceb about it later.

"Was it cold out?" Lin asked.

"No, I thought it would be colder," he said.

There was no answer. Jon raised himself to one elbow and looked at Lin. She was asleep.

He closed his eyes. It would be a long time yet until it was daylight, and he wanted to sleep.

Jon's thoughts faded into sleep and he began to dream a frightful dream of the dogs chasing him, rushing past him in their blindness, making him think he had escaped them, only to come again, always to come again. He opened his eyes and faced the darkness. It was better than the dreaming. He thought of the Fen on the platform. But there was something wrong, something that was all around him, and yet he couldn't see it. He forced his mind back to the Fen on the platform and tried to relive what he had seen.

Nothing. He closed his eyes again. In the darkness Lin's hand in his own was soft and comforting. He felt peaceful. Even Shadow was not ill-at-ease here. Shadow!

Quickly, he sat up. He had felt that there was something wrong. Now he knew what it was.

on reached for Lin and shook her gently.

"What is it?" she murmured sleepily.

"It's Jon," he said. "We have to leave!"

"Leave?" She moved against him as she adjusted her position. "Where? Why?"

"You asked me if it was cold outside and I said that it wasn't," he said. "But it had to be. It was snowing. And when I came back into the Compound my fingers were stiff, it had to be from the cold."

"I don't know what you're talking about," Lin said.

"There was snow on the ground outside," Jon said. "And Shadow seems cold."

"I'm not cold," Lin said. She took his hand. "Jon, are you all right?"

"You were cold before you took the sorpos!" he said. "Everyone here takes sorpos, it just makes them feel warm. No one gave Shadow sorpos, which is why he was cold. We've got to get out of here and head for the Ancient Land again. Are you well enough to leave now?"

She didn't answer but began stirring about, collecting her things. Jon went over to Ceb and started shaking him. Ceb pushed Jon's hand away twice before he woke.

"Ceb! Come outside with me!"

Ceb scratched the back of his neck and shook his head. Jon pulled him to his feet.

"What's wrong?"

"Come outside," Jon said in a loud voice.

He half led, half pulled Ceb to the middle of the Compound. Then he looked around and finally found the small gourd they used to drink water. He gave some water to Ceb, who drank it slowly. There was a small amount of water left in the gourd and Jon hoped it would begin to freeze to prove his point to Ceb.

"Ceb, you have to listen to me," he said. "This place is cold and getting colder. When the really cold weather hits, the Compound fence won't help you. It's the sorpos. The sorpos makes you think it's warm here."

"We can't leave here," Ceb said, shaking his head. "You have to stay here or the dogs are going to get you. I know what I'm talking about."

"Dogs? Then you know about the dogs?" Jon

asked. "And you mean you *know* it's cold in here? You know this and still you stay?"

"What are you looking for?" Ceb turned and started away. "We have a place here. . . ."

Jon followed Ceb, grabbed his arm, and spun him around. "Ceb, you're an Okalian!"

"Jon, you're making too much of this," Ceb said. "We've got plenty of time to . . . do whatever we have to do. Plenty of time."

Jon watched Ceb walk away. He stumbled after him in time to see him stretch out on the floor of the sleeping space. Pan and Atalia were sitting up. The lamp was on the floor between them. Pan touched her chest and lifted her hand to Jon. The sorpos was in it.

"They know it's getting colder," Lin said. "They know everything."

Jon turned away and picked up his tunic. A moment later he heard Kyra's voice and he knew Lin had awakened him. Jon went back outside to where Shadow waited.

A small figure waddled across the square, stopped at the water, and then waddled back to where it had come from.

"We're ready," Lin said.

Jon looked at Kyra's eyes and saw that they were wide, as if he were frightened.

"It'll be all right," Jon said to him.

It was growing somewhat lighter. From where they were, Jon could already make out the entrances of sleeping huts along the other side of the Compound. When they got to the entrance they found it guarded by a sleeping Fen.

Jon touched the heavy bolt across the door and then, with a heave, pushed it back. The Fen awoke with a start, wiped at his face, and grumbled as he reached for a torch that smoldered dimly. He blew on it until it flared up suddenly and held it above his head so that he could see the three of them. The Fen looked at Jon, and then Lin and Kyra.

Jon reached for the gate and the Fen put the torch close to him to examine his face. He said something, it might have been "Open gate," and Jon was surprised that he spoke Okalian. Ignoring the bright questioning eyes, Jon pushed the bolt. The Fen stepped toward Jon, puffing himself up and twisting his shoulders so that they slanted to one side, letting the torch go low so that it lit up his face from below.

In the time it took to lower the torch, Kyra had stepped toward him, pushing him back. Jon thought there would be a battle, right then and there.

There were footsteps behind them and the

Fen looked over Kyra's shoulder, holding up the torch again. It was Atun. He had a small bag under his arm.

"I'm going with you," he said.

The Fen turned toward Jon and looked at all of them again. Then he stepped aside.

They hadn't realized how still the air was within the Compound until they had stepped out of it. A cool breeze rushed across Jon's skin, and he felt clean and good.

"We'll have to be on the lookout for the dogs," he said.

They walked a short distance under the stars without knowing which way they were going and without speaking. Jon headed for high ground, hoping to see a direction they could take.

"It's getting colder," Kyra said.

"I know," Lin answered. She put her arm around his waist. It would be getting colder fast.

The cold would be their enemy, waiting for them to slow down, to falter. Jon thought about the dogs, yelping and whining and growling after them, unseeing, unknowing, uncaring, hungry.

The uphill climb was hard. Jon tired quickly and could hear Lin sucking the air between her teeth even though they were going slowly.

They hadn't been in the Compound long, but they all seemed weaker than before.

"Wait here," Jon said. "I'll go to the top and look over."

"We can all go up," Kyra said.

He started up and Shadow went with him. It was easier for Shadow. Jon went slowly, reaching for small branches to grab and pull himself along the steep incline. The sky was a dark bowl above him, filled with distant stars that threatened at any moment to come tumbling down and fall in a glorious heap about them. For a wild moment he felt he could leap up and reach them.

Shadow reached the top first and whinnied softly. He reared up, pawing the air. Jon got there a moment later with Kyra, and Lin and Atun followed. Atun sat down near a large rock and covered his head with his arms.

Jon knelt down beside him. "I'm glad you came."

"Is it true," Atun asked, without lifting his head, "that there is no Ancient Land?"

"Don't be silly." Jon shivered with the chill of the words that came from Atun and wondered how he could have held the weight of them as he labored up the mountainside. "Anyway, Ceb doesn't know as much as he pretends."

"He's my brother."

"Oh." Jon changed position. "Anyway, I'm glad you came, Atun."

Atun didn't answer, and Jon let him be and went to look around.

The other side of the crest dropped sharply, too sharply for them to try. But just beyond it was a high mesa that he knew must be Gunda's Hope. That was the place the Okalians thought would be the most challenging part of the journey from the Ancient Land to the new beginning that was Crystal City. They had looked at the mesa as a place of despair, but Gunda had called the Elders to a meeting, had joined hands with them, and then, lifting their hands together, had named the mesa Hope. And from that time on they had called it Gunda's Hope.

Behind them, to the north, Jon could see the Plain of Souls clearly. Off to the right he could see the twinkle of campfires, or perhaps they were just torches. It was hard to tell. Jon lined one of the fires up with his thumb for a long while to see if they were moving. They weren't. He wondered if they were Fens, or Okalians who had made it that far.

"Are they Okalians?" Lin's voice broke the silence, reading his thoughts.

Her face startled Jon as he turned toward her. She was paler than the moon, as if all of her life forces were being drained away slowly. She had grown thinner, so that her eyes looked much deeper in her head. Jon pushed away the hair from her face.

"I can't tell," he said.

"Why are the Okalians staying back there?" Lin asked. "What's wrong with them?"

"Atun said that Ceb doesn't believe there's an Ancient Land," Jon said. "If he doesn't have that hope, maybe he doesn't have a reason to go on."

"And what do you believe now?"

"That it's time for us to move on toward whatever it is we find," he said.

Lin grew weaker as they went along. Atun was just sad, and began to cry and to complain that they were going too fast. Jon lost his patience with him.

"Why don't you try being quiet!" he said.

"He's used to the sorpos," Lin said.

Atun stumbled along with his head down, staying as close to Kyra as he could.

In the daylight they could see Gunda's Hope clearly. They found a dark green swath that led up to the mesa flat and decided to follow it. They had pushed on for only a short time before Lin fell, sick and exhausted.

Jon picked Lin up and began to carry her,

but he knew he wasn't strong enough to go very far.

"Do you want me to carry her?" Kyra asked. He pushed the words out slowly, knowing he wouldn't be strong enough to carry his sister.

"No, maybe we can do something else," Jon said. He laid Lin carefully on the ground. "Do you have any food?"

Kyra looked first in the pouch he carried and pulled out a small piece of fruit. "Part of it is spoiled," he said.

"That may be all right," Jon said.

He took the fruit and looked around until he saw Shadow. He saw the animal and sensed the unicorn was aware of him. Without rising from his kneeling position, he held out his hand with the fruit in it.

"You think he'll carry her?" Atun asked.

"I don't know," Jon answered.

Shadow took a few tentative steps toward them, then stopped. Jon held the fruit higher. When the unicorn reached Jon, he took the fruit from his hand.

Standing, Jon put one hand carefully on the animal's neck.

"Please, Shadow," Jon whispered. "Please take her."

He knelt and lifted Lin's thin form in his arms. He placed her across Shadow's broad back and watched as the girl put both arms around the unicorn's neck.

They traveled all day. Jon pushed one foot in front of the other until his legs ached and he was so tired he had to think about each step. Push a foot forward. Then the next. Then the next. They saw the dogs once. First they heard their yelping and then they saw them far off to the left. The gray huddle was moving away from them. They watched for a while and then moved on, too tired to make much of it.

Atun trailed them and Jon thought it might have been a mistake to bring him along. But what if they had left the boy behind? He was still an Okalian while the others were, somehow, no longer Okalians. They had given themselves up to the sorpos. It warmed them and told them that their home was warm, and that life was good, and that there was no purpose except the peace the sorpos brought them.

Kyra was always ahead of Jon, next to Shadow and his sister. He had put the marks on his face again. Sometimes, as he walked, Jon saw him swing his head from side to side.

There are nightmares in his head, Jon thought. They whispered to him and he answered with a hunching of his shoulders, a twisting of his body. Kyra was changing, and the other Okalians in the Compound had changed, too. They were away from Crystal City, and from the rules that told them who they were.

They moved on until they found a small stream. There was ice floating in the middle of it and long crystals along the side. Soon it would be frozen. Kyra brought water to Lin and she drank it. Jon watched her throat moving as she swallowed. When she had finished drinking she smiled at him, and the curve of her lips was beautiful and gentle.

"Will we stay here for the night?" Kyra asked.

"Can you stay alone?" Jon asked him.

Kyra looked at Jon and then quickly away.

"I want to get help for Lin," Jon said. "You can stay with her while Shadow, Atun, and I go for help. Otherwise, I'm afraid . . . I'm afraid for her."

"She'll be all right," Kyra said. His eyes were filled with tears.

"Can you stay with her?"

Kyra nodded.

They waited until it was dark, and then Jon told Atun what he planned to do. Atun put his head down and said it wouldn't work. Jon said he would do it anyway, and Atun could stay with Lin and Kyra if he wished. Atun said he would go along.

on remembered the Fens passing them, heading in the direction of Bemen's Plateau. Back at Crystal City he would have gone to one of the Elders who had been trained in medicine, but out here the only thing he could think of was to find a Fen camp and look for their healing herbs.

"It won't work," Atun said. "They won't give them to you."

"I'm not going to ask them," Jon said. "I'm . . . just going to take the herbs if I can find them."

"That's wrong," Atun said.

"If you think it's wrong then you should stay here," Jon said.

Atun scowled. "I'll go."

They walked on until Jon saw the flickering of Fen campfires in the distance. He pointed them out to Atun and they headed toward them. The fires looked very far away at first, until Jon realized that he and Atun were walking through a small valley. Once out of the valley they could look down on the fires, which were along a hillside.

"It won't take us long to get there," Jon said. "Let's go, but keep a lookout for Fens."

"Will you attack them?"

"I'll defend myself if I have to," Jon said.

"What does that mean?"

"Whatever it has to mean," Jon said. "Lin is very sick."

"It's okay if you tell me what to do," Atun continued. "I'm just a child."

"How old are you?"

"Nine."

"You'll be all right," Jon said. "Don't worry."

Jon didn't want to tell Atun what to do. He didn't want to be responsible for him. But he knew what Atun wanted. He wanted to be a child again, as he had been back at Crystal City. In the Wilderness it was hard to be a child.

"I didn't see any Fen children," Jon said as he started again toward the fires.

"There were Fen children at the Compound," Atun said. "Their parents weren't really old, though."

"I think they were as old as Ceb," Jon said. "I didn't think they would even be that old."

As they neared the Fen camp they could hear

the sounds of the Fen flutes in the wind, and once in a while they could see one of the Fens silhouetted against a fire. There was a strong smell in the air, and Jon thought that it was something the Fens were burning to keep the dogs away.

Jon didn't know if the Fens had posted guards. He hoped that they would be like himself, afraid of what they could not see, lighting their fires so the darkness would not seem so near, so menacing.

"Be quiet."

Off to their left a branch, caught by the wind, whisked across the ground. It wasn't a dog. They waited for a long moment and then continued.

"We never played games at the Compound," Atun said in a whisper.

"Did you play games at Crystal City?"

"Yes, a lot of games," Atun answered.

"I used to like to play games," Jon said. "My mother wanted to play all the time."

"I think about my mother sometimes," Atun said. "She's really pretty. Like Atalia."

"Shh!" Jon said. "You want to let every Fen in the world know we're here?"

He didn't want to think about Atun's mother, or his own. He didn't want to think about games they used to play back in Crystal City, or anything else. He just wanted to find a Fen with the herbs they used for healing. He didn't know how he would get them from the Fen, only that he had to get them.

When they reached the edge of the Fen camp, Jon told Atun to stay behind.

"I'm going to try to sneak into their camp and look for the herbs," Jon said. "Stay here. If you think that something went wrong . . . go back and tell the others."

"Suppose you can't find herbs?"

"I'll find them," Jon said. "Don't worry about it."

Jon moved along the edge of the camp. He could actually see the Fens now, huddled together, sometimes with their arms around one another. He looked around until he saw one lying alone.

The lone Fen slept on his back with both arms stretched out. Next to him there was a dark form that Jon thought might have been another Fen. From where he crouched, Jon could see two pouches tied to a cord lying on the Fen's heaving chest. He glanced over at Atun, saw that the boy was watching him, and then began slowly crawling toward the Fen.

Asleep, the Fen looked more like a child than any of them did awake. Jon watched as the Fen's chest rose and fell. He looked to see if the

Fen had a weapon and saw that there was a bit of cloth around one wrist. He was sure now that the Fen was a girl. The dark form was a large skin, or maybe several joined together.

The Fen's mouth was open and Jon could see that her teeth were dark. Sorpos. He moved close to the sleeping Fen, trying not to make a noise. Carefully he opened one of the pouches. It contained bits of sorpos. The other one was half filled with a green powder. He was about to untie the pouch with the herbs when he heard the sound of high voices behind him.

Two Fens were coming toward him. Jon ducked his head close to the Fen. Quickly he pulled the skin over his shoulders and tucked his legs near his chest. In the darkness under the stinking skin Jon tried to be still, tried to keep himself from shaking with fear. He could feel his heart beating in his temples as the voices came near him.

The Fen voices were over him now. A cold trickle of sweat ran down the side of his face and onto his neck. He felt something step over him and then heard a grunting sound inches from his ear. Then nothing.

For a long time he lay still, not daring to move. He clenched his teeth and fists hard, and opened them again slowly.

The thought came to him that the Fens might have stopped near him, and were just waiting for him to come out from under the skin. Or maybe they had left. Slowly he pulled the smelly skin away from his face. He turned his head to see if anything was behind him. Nothing. In the distance a thin line of dark clouds rolled quickly past the pale moon. The fire near the center of the camp had died down.

Jon sat up and looked at the Fen lying next to him. One of the pouches was gone. Jon quickly took the other from the string and moved away. He looked inside. It was the herbs. The other Fens had taken the sorpos.

He crawled away and almost stepped on another sleeping Fen. He carefully took both of his pouches and then started making his way back to where he had left Shadow and Atun.

"EEE! EEEE! EEEEE!"

The sound sent chills through his body. He looked up and saw a Fen standing over him. The Fen held a stick — it could have been a spear — high over his head. Jon pushed himself forward as fast as he could, grabbing at the Fen's legs. He felt the Fen grab at the back of his neck as they went sprawling into the dirt.

The Fen grabbed his leg and Jon kicked out with his free leg. He kicked him again and again and the Fen rolled away. Jon got to his feet quickly and for a moment he couldn't see the Fen.

"Jon! Jon!" It was Atun.

"EEEEEE! EEEEEEE!" The Fen had moved away and was jumping up and down, trying to wake the other Fens.

Jon began to run; he saw Atun and they ran together. He looked over his shoulder and saw that there were torches being lit behind him at the Fen camp, but none were moving in his direction.

Jon was exhausted. It was even difficult to take one breath after another. "Let's go," he said.

"I saw you fighting that Fen," Atun was saying. "You're very strong. You should be our leader. You can tell us all what to do."

Atun lifted Jon's arm and put it around his own shoulders.

"You all right?" Jon asked.

"Sure," Atun said. "I didn't know you could fight like that. You knocked that Fen down like it was nothing, right?"

Jon didn't answer. He was close to crying. Tears came so quickly now, so easily. He remembered his father once had said he was very brave, that he had outgrown tears. He had fallen and hurt his elbow. He had wanted to cry but knew that his father didn't like to see him give in to pain, so he had held back the tears. His father had put his arm around Jon's shoulders, the same way his arm was now around Atun's shoulders, and told him how brave he was. Later, alone in his bed, he had cried.

Atun kept talking about how brave he had been, and how he had knocked down the Fen. It was the first time he had ever tried to hurt anything in his life. He hadn't been brave, he had been desperate, and so filled with fear that he had struck out at the Fen with all his strength. The Fen had been startled to find him there and couldn't have seen him very well in the darkness. Jon knew if the Fen had seen his face he would have seen the panic in his eyes, the horror in his face.

He hadn't seen the Fen very well, either. All he had seen in the hurried flicker of shadows was something he feared.

"Kyra was afraid you weren't coming back," Lin said. She seemed so weak. Her shoulders formed a fragile bow that held her body barely safe from the wind. "I told him you would be back."

Jon offered her the pouch.

"I don't know what it will do," he said. "I've only heard . . ."

"Thank you, Jon." Lin smiled and touched her cheek to his hand. Her face was warm but her hands were cold.

Jon thought the herbs would help Lin, but he also thought she needed rest. Not just to be still, or to sleep, but to have the peace of knowing everything would be all right in the next day, the next hour, the next breath. That would be real rest.

"Jon fought with one of the Fens," Atun said before Jon could stop him. "He stopped his dreaming."

Lin turned to Jon quickly, searching his face. "You did what?"

"I didn't stop his dreaming," he answered, angrily. "Look, we'd better get going. In case they're following us."

"Are you all right?" Lin asked.

Kyra came close.

"Yes, I just . . . we were both surprised to see each other. I don't think that . . . it was very quick. I don't think I hurt him."

"You can stop a Fen's dreaming?" Kyra asked. There was something childlike in his voice.

"I wouldn't want to," Jon said. "Now, let's get moving."

The wind wasn't as strong, but it was colder. They walked with Lin hunched on Shadow's back, Kyra walking ahead, and Atun following him single file. Jon brought up the rear, his shoulders aching from tensing them against the bitter chill.

They walked through the night and into the next day, stopping for only a few minutes now and again when either Kyra or Atun was too tired to go on. There were times when Jon was too tired to go on, times when the frozen ground would send shards of pain through his feet and his fingers would curl with the cold and he had to push one hand against the other to straighten them out.

Atun came up beside Jon and touched his shoulder. Jon looked at him and saw him point toward a small hill to the left. It would be shelter against the wind. Jon nodded, and led Shadow toward it.

The ground was too hard to leave footprints and Jon doubted if any Fens were around. There was a dark area off to one side and Jon thought it might be a cave.

"Kyra, help Lin off Shadow," Jon said. "I want to look around."

Kyra nodded grimly.

Cautiously, Jon went to the dark area he had seen. It was a cave. He found a rock and threw it in, then another. There was no response.

Lin didn't want to move from where she was lying on the ground. Jon thought if she fell asleep there it would be bad. He told them about the cave and they struggled into it.

They settled Lin just inside the mouth of the cave, and Atun and Jon went out again to look for dry sticks. They found some that were dry and others that were damp but took them all the same. The idea of a fire appealed to Jon.

Jon hoped he could remember how to start a fire with stones. With Atun sheltering him from the wind, he banged the rocks together over a small pile of dry leaves. It took him long minutes to get it started, but finally they had a small blaze. Jon put in one end of a stick until it caught, then stamped out the rest of the fire.

They got back to the cave and decided to try to find their way farther in before lighting a larger fire, so that the smoke wouldn't give them away. They made their way in the darkness with Atun in the lead and Kyra and Lin following. For some reason Shadow wouldn't go into the cave. Jon thought he might come in later.

They moved as far back into the cave as they dared, not really wanting to get too far from the opening.

The cave was warm. Atun and Jon put the dry sticks and some leaves they had gathered in a pile and lit them.

"I feel a small breeze," Atun said. "Maybe there's another opening somewhere."

Jon lit one of the sticks and held it up. The cave was huge, much larger than he thought it would be. It seemed to go down forever. He looked up at the path they had used to climb down into the cave. It was narrow and twisted along the nearly yellow walls of the cave.

The smoke from the fire went to the right and collected in a small pocket. It was possible that it would get smoky in the cave, but that was all right. For the moment, they were out of the cold.

"Shadow didn't come in?" Atun asked.

"No, but it's okay," Jon said. "We'll just rest here a while, maybe get some sleep, and then we'll move on. We'll find him again."

In the glow of the small fire, Jon could see Lin's face. She was pretty. He thought about what they would do when they reached the Ancient Land. He had asked his father what they would do, and his father had said that he would have to find a mate. He wondered if Lin thought that he would be a good mate.

"Jon." It was Lin's voice. "Where do you think we are?"

"Gunda's Hope," he answered. "I'm sure of it. When we get past here it'll be a short journey to the Swarm Mountains."

"Then up rose Puc!" Kyra said, quoting from the Book of Orenllag.

"Then up rose Puc!" Jon repeated, closing his eyes.

He fell asleep quickly.

In a dream the Fen he had fought was lying on the ground and, for some reason, Jon sat nearby watching him. The Fen lay motionless as Jon watched. After a long time he stirred, lifting a huge arm to shield his eyes from the sun. The Fen looked around, dazed, and began to grope around the ground for his weapon. Still, in the dream, Jon was motionless. Even when the Fen had wrapped his fingers around the spear and was getting to his feet, Jon was unable to move. But now he saw his face. It was the same one he had fought. The Fen screamed at him, the sound hurting his ears. Jon screamed back. It was the same sound.

"Jon! Jon!"

Jon felt his shoulder being shaken and he felt something pushing against his legs. He opened his eyes and saw that it was dark except for the small pile of glowing ashes in front of him. For a moment he didn't know where he was. Then he remembered the cave.

"What is it?" he asked.

"Lin thinks we should move on." It was

Atun's voice. "She thinks there are dogs in the back of the cave."

"See if you can build up the fire," Jon said.

"I'm scared! I'm scared!" Atun's voice was high and wavery.

The sound of a dog yelping was no more than a few meters away.

The fire flared up as Atun stirred it. Jon could see Lin clearly now, the flames lighting her face from below, giving her an eerie look. He looked around. There was only one dog near them.

"The others are over there," Lin's voice cracked as she spoke. "He's looking for us."

Jon looked and saw the sightless, glowing eyes of the other dogs, and the moving mass that was their bodies. He took a stick and lit the end of it and pushed it toward the dog that was near them. The dog moved away from the smell of the smoking stick, howling.

"The others are beginning to move this way!" Kyra called.

Jon took the stick and pushed it closer to the dog. The animal growled and lifted its head. It bared its teeth and bit at the air. Then it lowered its head and pushed forward, trying to contact whatever was near it. Jon pushed the flame against the dog and watched it recoil. The dog moved away, crouching so its belly was touching the ground.

Jon looked up and saw the other dogs still moving toward them, pushing into each other, lifting their heads to find the odor of the intruders. He pushed the stick as hard as he could into the dog's side. The dog turned and attacked the stick and Jon held it against the dog's side as hard as he could. The dog rolled over and started yelping in pain. Its fur was on fire.

The other dogs, signaled by the change in tone of the yelps, stopped, and began howling in a high pitch that Jon had never heard before.

The dog that was burning ran in a small circle, twisting back onto himself trying to bite whatever was causing him the pain. Finally he got back to the pack.

The howling stopped, and the yelps began again, and the growling that signaled they were about to attack. Jon held the flame high and watched as the dogs attacked the one that he had set afire. In moments it was over. They had killed it.

They bunched together and edged toward the mouth of the cave. Behind them the dogs fought their way through the huge pile to tear at the injured animal. Jon pushed Lin ahead of him.

"I can't see where I'm going!" Lin said.

"Just stay close to the wall."

It seemed to take forever until Lin said that she thought they had reached the mouth of the cave.

"Be sure!" Jon said.

The echo of the words had barely died when an icy gust of wind hit them.

They scrambled outside, Kyra falling and rolling part of the way down the hill. The wind drove Jon backward, taking his breath. He took Lin's hand. She leaned forward and gritted her teeth as the wind whipped her hair into her face. At the bottom of the hill they looked for Shadow.

It was Lin who saw the unicorn silhouetted against the distant moon.

They started again, trying to push ahead faster as the wind picked up. Bits of debris tore into Jon's face and he found himself leaning far forward just to stay on his feet. Behind them they heard yelping. The dogs were out of the cave.

They were in a dust squall and Jon could taste the dust in his mouth. He had seen the squalls when he was in Crystal City, darkening the skies and covering everything in their path. Sometimes, when the wind shifted, the thick clouds of dust seemed to leap into the air like some great monster. From within the walls of the city it had been a wondrous sight, but he was not in the city and the sand and dirt cut into his skin and choked his breathing. Jon turned and saw the dogs headed back toward the cave.

They went on until they came to a small stand of trees. They all sank to the ground near them. Jon thought about the dogs, imagining the beasts huddled against the dust storm even as the Okalians were. He closed his eyes, shielded his face the best he could, and let the wind do what it would. It was not just his body that was tired, it was his soul.

It took forever for the dust storm to stop, or

at least it seemed forever. Jon lay gasping on his side. He looked over to where Lin crouched. He tried crawling to her but his hands, cut and bruised from climbing down the rock, were too sore to move along the ground.

"Lin!"

She didn't answer, just raised a thin hand.

When the dust settled they all looked terrible. Kyra looked the worst as he stood panting against a dead tree, the whites of his eyes peering from the black grime on his face. Lin was trying to get some sticks from her hair. Jon went to see Atun and found him clinging to a small tree. He looked unconscious. Jon knelt to examine him. Gently he moved the boy's arm from his face. His eyes were barely open. There was moisture on his face as well as dirt. A small cut on his brow formed a perfect crescent over his left eye. Jon looked at his mouth. At first he thought it was bleeding. He pushed the red lips back. Sorpos!

There was a pouch next to him and Jon didn't have to open it to know what it contained.

When everyone had recovered, Jon realized they weren't as bad off as he had thought they would be. They had accomplished a small victory over both the dogs and the dust. Lin managed a smile, and even Kyra, once he had cleaned himself up and had started grumbling about the dogs, seemed in fair spirits.

"We'll have to carry wood for torches," Lin said. "It works against the dogs."

"And hope they all avoid the smell of smoke," Jon said.

"You can fight them," Kyra said to Jon. His eyes were narrowed into slits and Jon thought he had put even more marks on his face. "You can stop their dreaming — the Fens and the dogs."

"I didn't stop the dreaming of the Fen —" Jon said. He felt his face flush. "I did *not* kill the Fen."

"Maybe the other Fens killed him when they saw that you had beat him," Kyra said. "Like the dogs. The other dogs killed the one you beat."

Jon turned to answer Kyra, but he saw the boy wasn't talking to him anymore. He was having a conversation with himself, rocking to and fro, nodding as he agreed with his own vision of what had happened. Jon looked at Lin, and she went to Kyra and put her arms around him.

They started walking again. Atun kept off to himself, and Jon felt that was good because he didn't want to speak with him. As they walked, they rechecked their course.

They decided to rest when Atun spotted a small stream. They weren't sure if it was clean, so they used its waters to wash themselves as best they could and chewed on plants along the edge of the stream for moisture.

They decided that Lin and Kyra would sleep while Atun and Jon kept watch. Jon had thought that Kyra would not sleep, that he would pace as usual, but he did sleep, breathing heavily and tossing about as he did. Jon sat next to Atun and asked him how he was doing. He didn't answer.

"I know what you have in the pouch," Jon said.

"I don't care," Atun answered. "I'm going back to the Compound anyway."

"You'd be lost if you went back," Jon said. "Especially with that stuff."

"Ceb was right," Atun said. "We should just find a safe place to be."

"The Book of Orenllag says that there is an Ancient Land," Jon said. "Do you believe Ceb or the book?"

"I don't know what to believe anymore!"

"Atun, if you're going to stay with us you have to do without the sorpos," Jon said. He searched for something more to say to Atun, something comforting, but nothing came.

Atun fell asleep and Jon let him. Somewhere

between worrying about Atun and wondering if they were still going in the right direction, he fell asleep himself. When he woke, he found Lin sitting over him. She had pulled his head into her lap and was smoothing his hair with her hands.

"It's only me," Lin said. "I thought you would want to know that Shadow is back."

Jon lifted his head and saw Shadow. His legs were covered with dust and dirt.

"He just got here a few minutes ago," Lin said. "I tried to get near him, but he shied away. He's getting wilder."

"How long have I been asleep?"

"Not long," she said.

"Are you all right?"

Lin put her arm around Jon's shoulder and put her cheek against his. "No," she said. "I'm out here in the Wilderness, and I'm tired and cold and hungry. But maybe it's not as bad as it could be."

"Sounds pretty bad."

"I have you," Lin answered. "It could be worse."

It was warmer.

"There's something coming!" It was Kyra's voice.

Jon felt Lin move away and he sat up at once.

There, clearly silhouetted against the horizon, a hooded figure rode toward them. The figure was on a large, humpbacked ox.

"What are we going to do?" Lin called to Jon. She was leaning forward, straining to see what was coming.

"Wait for it, whatever it is," he said. It was moving toward them very quickly.

Shadow pranced about and reared up.

Jon looked beyond the figure and saw nothing. Whatever it was, there was only one of it. It slowed as it came nearer and Jon could see that it was large. There was a hood the color of dried blood and a cape to match. Beneath the hood and cape were other colors and cloths. Jon couldn't tell where the cloths stopped and the person, if it was indeed a person, began.

It stopped. For a while it didn't move, and then it came slowly into the clearing in front of them. An arm went up and the hood was pulled away. There was a face that could have been Okalian if it had been less tortured, if the eyes had been less piercing.

"Who are you?" Jon called out.

"Who are you?" the figure repeated in a low, strange voice.

"I am Jon, of the Okalians," Jon answered.

"I am Jon, of the Okalians," the visitor said, and laughed.

Silence. Birds flew to the ground and pecked at fruit that Lin had dropped.

"What do you want?" Jon said.

"What do you want?" was the reply.

Silence.

"We are looking for the Ancient Land of our people," Jon said. "The land of the Okalians."

The figure breathed deeply, and exhaled slowly.

"I am the Soo, the Fire Bearer." The figure produced from beneath his robes a brass ball from which came wisps of smoke. "Perhaps you have need of fire? The price is good."

"We have nothing with which to pay."

"Pity! Pity!" he said. "But perhaps you will allow me to have my meal with you?"

Before Jon could answer, the stranger leaped nimbly from the ox and, taking sticks that he had bound to the side of the animal, began building a fire. First he made a pyramid of small sticks, then he placed larger ones over it. He took the brass ball and swung it around the pile several times before stopping it. Then he took the top off the ball and placed a small stick in it. The stick began to burn and he placed it quickly beneath the pile.

"Sit," he said. His voice was friendly.

He took off his cape and some of the things he wore beneath it. Some were cloth and some were the skins of animals.

"I'm glad that you aren't Fens," he said. "They are not trusting. Okalians are always trusting."

"Do you know many Okalians?" Lin asked at once.

"A few," the Soo said. "A few pass this way now and again."

"Do you know where they go?" Jon asked.

"Where do they go? Where do they go? It's a very good question," he said.

The fire crackled and flickered, sending its warmth to all of them. It seemed like a friend that he had brought along.

"Who are you?" Lin asked. "What are you?"

"What am I?" he asked. He pulled at his shaggy beard. "I am the Soo, the Fire Bearer. It is what I do and who I am. Here there is cold that creeps and kills. It is fire that holds it off."

He swung the brass ball about, leaving a wispy trail of smoke in the air.

"Here there are dogs that follow the scent of warm blood," he continued. "It is the fire that drives them off."

The Soo sat facing the fire, his pale and scaly legs crossed, staring into the blaze.

"Are you hungry?" the Soo asked, pulling out a pouch from his garments and unwrapping it. In the pouch there were leaves with pieces of a purplish stem still attached. No one admitted to being hungry.

"You say you have seen others like us," Lin spoke slowly, deliberately. "Do you know of the Ancient Land of the Okalians?"

"The Okalians?" The Soo pulled out a wide metal blade with which he scraped his legs. "They pass from time to time, going where they go. Weren't they the ones that fled when the Beasts attacked the Swarm?"

"You don't know anything." Atun walked away from the fire.

"It was the Okalians who rose from the Swarm," Jon said.

"One time," the Soo went on as if there had been no interruptions, "in a land far, far from here, there was a strange but happy tribe. They had learned many useful things. Nice things. Nice things. They invented a way to bring the heat of fire to cold places. They invented a way to take water to the places where there is no water. Then they had the nicest idea of all. They invented themselves. You should have seen how they enjoyed that invention."

"You can't invent yourself," Jon said.

"No? That's not true?" the Soo looked up at Jon. One eye nearly closed beneath the shaggy white hair. "As I grow old I have trouble knowing what is true. They did not invent themselves?"

"Of course not," Lin said.

"But none of this was important to this tribe. Nice, but not important. In seasons past there were many ways to do things and none was more important than the other. Then, one day, as many seasons past as there are stars in the sky . . ."

"How do you know this?" Kyra said.

Jon looked at Kyra and he looked down at the ground before him. "Let the Soo speak," Jon said.

"Ahh, let the Soo speak," the Soo said.

"Tell us more about this tribe," Jon said,

when the Soo seemed more absorbed in his scratching than anything else.

"One day," the Soo went on, "some of the tribe were alone, waiting for the others to return to their camp. The ones who waited were on a high hill, higher than the nests of the great birds. It was a place in which they thought they would be safe from other animals who might eat them. Did I tell you they did not like being eaten?"

"I had guessed it," Lin said. She smiled.

"Possible," the Soo said. "At any rate, there were nine of these creatures on the hill. Those who had left the camp were many times that number. Maybe even more. After a great while those on the hill saw, off in the distance, those returning from the hunt for grains, which was what they ate — that and a little fruit for the bowels."

Jon looked at Atun. He was bringing his hands to his mouth in a way so no one could see what he was doing. Jon knew it was the sorpos again. Lin had her arm about Kyra and Jon moved closer to them, away from Atun.

"One of them saw off in the distance, opposite of where they were, a frightening sight," the Soo went on. "It was the Beasts. Big things with curved teeth that ate everything."

"You mean the dogs?" Lin asked.

"Bigger than the dogs. Many times bigger than the dogs. It was the Beasts that drove the dogs into the caves where they lost their sight. No, the Beasts were nightmares with five legs and twenty teeth, maybe forty teeth. Who knows?"

"Five legs?"

"Maybe seven, maybe three. But they attacked this great swarm of a tribe that wanted only to live with quiet hearts. They attacked, and all the tribe stayed together bravely to fight them off except for one small group that ran off."

"What are you talking about?" Jon asked. "Are you talking about the Swarm? Have you read the Book of Orenllag?"

"I don't think the Soo reads," Lin said.

"I bear fire, not words," the Soo said. "But words are good, a comfort that can be shared. Not as great a comfort as fire, but a comfort."

"You speak of a land far away." Lin pushed herself forward on her knees. "Do you know where this land is?"

"Are there other tribes still around?" Jon asked.

"There is the Soo." The Soo touched his chest. "The Soo is of the Kargs. There are so few of us. It is sad. There are tales of the Na'ans, but I have never met any of them."

"They are written of in the Book of Oren-llag," Jon said. "They are a tribe."

"Then there are the Fens," the Soo said. "The Fens are not a trusting tribe."

"Where is this place that the Beasts attacked the tribe you speak of?" Jon asked.

"I have heard it was that way," the Soo said, pointing in the direction of the Crystal City.

Jon turned away. "I don't think so," he said.

"Do you always travel alone?" Lin asked.

"Alone? Yes, alone. The fire doesn't speak to me. I listen, but it doesn't speak." The Soo held up the brass ball. "Would you like the fire? Would you like to be a fire bearer? I will give it to you in exchange for one of the boys. Whichever one talks the most. I'll teach him to be a fire bearer."

"We're Okalians," Lin said. "We don't give each other away."

"Pity, it's such a good trade," the Soo said, grinning. He scratched again at the silvery scales on his legs. "Nothing can live in the Wilderness long without fire. You can't. I am the Soo, and I can't."

"We'll take the fire from you!" Kyra said.

Jon looked at Kyra. His teeth were clenched and his face tightened so that Jon could hardly recognize him. The boy hurled himself across the space between him and the Soo and sent the old man tumbling backward.

"Kyra!" Lin screamed at her brother.

Kyra and the Soo tumbled over in a mass of rags and bare legs. Jon saw the blade that the Soo had been using to scrape his legs and picked it up quickly.

The Soo pushed Kyra aside and sprang quickly to his feet. He saw Jon standing with the blade and his dark eyes rolled about from one of them to the other. The brass ball of fire was on the ground between them.

"Jon stopped a Fen's dreaming," Kyra shouted from where he lay. "He'll stop yours!"

The Soo looked at Jon and pointed a bony, yellow-nailed finger. "You?"

Jon knew it wasn't true, but he nodded anyway.

"You want to take the fire from me." The Soo spoke quietly, almost sadly.

"You said we can't live without it," Lin said.

"And you are Okalians?"

"We are Okalians," Jon said.

The Soo took a step toward the brass ball, but Kyra beat him to it and kicked it toward Jon. The Soo looked at Jon, looked into his eyes, and down to the blade he held in his hand.

"He's afraid of us!" Kyra said.

"There's no need to be afraid of us," Jon said. "We don't need his fire. We are Okalians. We can make our own fire."

He threw the blade to the ground at the Soo's feet. The Soo bent quickly and picked up the blade and the brass ball that contained the fire. His lips were thin and pink, and when he pursed them to blow on the fire he looked like some wild animal that had managed to stand erect and to wrap itself in the tattered disguise of a higher creature.

The smoke came from the ball in a small blue cloud, then narrowed to a wisp, which pleased the Soo. He wrapped his face again.

"Yes, you are truly Okalians, wandering along the edges of your darkness," he said, his voice raspy and low. "Is this the darkness you dream in?"

"We are Okalians," Kyra said. "The people who dream greatly."

"The people who dream greatly," the Soo repeated.

"He's afraid of us," Kyra said again.

"It's time for us to leave now," Jon said, stepping in front of Kyra.

"Which way?" Lin asked. "The Soo pointed back to Crystal City."

"The way we know," Jon said. "Come on."

He put his arm around Kyra and started off. Lin walked behind them and Atun followed.

Jon turned to see what the Soo was doing. He saw that he had settled again in front of his fire, rocking to and fro. From a short distance away he looked like an incredibly old man in front of a fire, and from a farther distance like merely a pile of rags, and from still farther like a fire whose smoke had failed to rise and had settled next to its own flame for warmth.

As they walked, Jon thought about the Book of Orenllag. He told himself that what was written there was true, it was the Okalians who had risen from the Swarm and become a great people. They had not run away, but had been led by the great Puc, and had risen. Had truly risen.

They had reached the far end of Gunda's Hope, the vast mesa over which the Okalians had struggled on their way northward to the area in which they would build Crystal City, so long ago. They had climbed down the mesa, holding on to the small trees that dotted the far side. It was evening when they reached the ground below and the Red Moon of the Okalians hung in all its fullness and beauty in the distance. The Red Moon heartened them, even as the sprinkling of trees on the mesa side had. It was warmer on this side of Gunda's Hope, and more trees and plants were growing. Jon felt it was a good sign. But from the edge of the mesa they had also seen how far they had to go. The Swarm Mountains, dark and forbidding, were at least a day ahead; to their left and even more distant there was a tiny patch of blue green that Jon saw and hoped in his heart was the lake of Orenllag.

They decided to sleep. They found tall grass and found places in it. Jon was the last to lie down, looking around first to see if there were any signs of danger. He didn't see any and allowed himself to stretch out completely on the ground, looking up at the darkening skies. He fell asleep thinking about the Soo. He told himself over and over that he didn't care what the Soo had said. The old man had challenged the Book of Orenllag, had given his own version of how the Okalians had faced the Beasts and how the Okalians had fled to save themselves. It wasn't true, Jon told himself. The Soo didn't know how Okalians had always risen, had always learned to dream greatly. It was the reason they had built Crystal City, to keep creatures like the Soo out. The Soo and the Fens.

Lin moved from where she was lying and came near enough to Jon to take his hand.

"How are you doing?" he asked.

"I'm tired, as usual," she answered, then lifted his hand to her mouth and kissed it gently.

Jon couldn't sleep as long as Lin held his hand. It was only when she had fallen asleep and had released his hand that he finally drifted off.

He woke up with a start and looked about

him. The air was damp, still. Lin was asleep not far from him, her body angled oddly, her fingers spread against the ground as if she felt for its warmth. Jon watched her for a while, seeing her stretch in her sleep, thinking she was beautiful. Kyra was near her feet. He moved about uneasily in his sleep, jerking his head from side to side. He reached out with his hand until he touched Lin's bare leg just below the knee. Then, holding it, he became calm again.

Jon sat up slowly. What was it that he was sensing? He looked around, squinting into the semidarkness, until he saw a movement in the shadows. For a moment he froze and then, slowly, he began to recognize the shape and knew what was happening. It was Atun, preparing to leave.

Jon couldn't see his features, but he saw when Atun stood and looked about. Jon let him go a short distance and then went after him, catching him just beyond the little camp they had made.

"Why?" Jon asked.

"Ceb needs me."

"He doesn't need you or anybody else."

"He does," Atun protested. "You don't know."

"He has the sorpos," Jon said. "What does he need you for?"

Atun turned away and started on.

"I think you're going back for the sorpos."

Atun whirled toward Jon, his face twisted and angry, his thin shoulders hunched forward. "You don't know anything!" he hissed. "You don't know anything!"

His teeth were dark at the edges. Jon knew he had been at the sorpos again. "You won't make it back," Jon said. "The Fens will catch you before you get past Gunda's Hope."

"I'll make it back," he said quietly.

"Atun." Jon spoke gently to him as he backed away. "There's no real life in the Compound. They're living in a made-up world. You have to know that."

"Maybe that's better," Atun said. "I don't know."

He half walked, half stumbled off, looking frail and small in the great Wilderness.

When Lin and Kyra woke, Jon told them that Atun had left. Lin cupped her elbows in her hands. She began to cry, loud sobbing that shook her whole body. Jon put his arms around her and held her until she had recovered. She pushed away from him and stood. Her mouth tightened and she rubbed her face briskly with the palms of her hands.

"We had better start again," she said.

Kyra looked off in the direction that Atun

had gone. He rubbed his own face, as his sister had, smearing the markings.

Jon knew that they weren't so concerned with Atun's leaving, or even with the fact that he might not make it back to the Compound — they all had doubts that any of them would make it to safety.

They hadn't seen Shadow for a while. Jon pictured him running freely through the Wilderness, finding his strength in freedom, his joy in the wind racing past his head.

Beneath their feet was a tangled mass of dead material that forced them to lift their legs higher than they would normally. But there were also green buds that pushed up as well, living material rising from the dead. Jon tried to remember the passages from the Book of Orenllag that would tell them where they were. They would soon reach the Swarm Mountains, and if they climbed one of them they might even be able to see the Ancient Land.

Lin walked closer to Jon. When they had started, she had always stayed closer to Kyra.

"Those low clouds over the mountains are really dark," Jon said. "You think it might rain?"

"I don't feel like talking," Lin said.

"Is something wrong?"

"It's just too hard," she said. "It's all too hard. Just be quiet and keep going."

Jon glanced at her out of the corner of his eyes. She was strained; they were all strained. He walked faster, knowing that she would have to work harder to catch up, not knowing why he would want to make her work harder. After a while he slowed and looked at her, and she returned his look with defiance.

Later, when he stopped and said it was time to rest, it was Lin who ignored him and walked on. He had already sat down and had to get up to follow her.

Kyra, always behind them, had begun to mumble to himself.

The next day was a nightmare of pain and confusion. Jon couldn't tell if they walked more, or if they spent most of their time lying on the ground. When the sun had almost gone down, outlining the mountaintops with golden halos, they found a berry bush. It lifted their spirits, and they sat around the bush and ate as much as they could.

"You have berry juice all over your face," Kyra said to Lin.

Lin responded by rubbing the berries into her face and licking off the juice with a smile.

"There's nothing like food to make you feel good," Jon said.

"Makes me feel good," Lin said.

"Me, too," Kyra said. "I didn't eat much back

in Crystal City but now I think about food a lot."

"I think we all do," Jon said. "We have to make peace with food, and with the weather, and with each other."

Lin held out a handful of berries to Jon. "But when you have food it is easier to make the peace," she said.

That night they all slept soundly.

It was late in the morning when Jon awoke. Lin had gathered some more berries for them to carry, and Kyra had painted his face again, this time using the juice from the berries to make the markings darker. Lin seemed in a good mood.

They were talking about a dance Lin had learned in Crystal City when they heard sounds drifting toward them from the distance. The hills nearby were not really the start of the Swarm Mountains, but they were high enough to see for some distance.

"Wait here," Jon said.

He ran up the hill as fast as he could and found a small ledge. He looked down to where Kyra and Lin were watching him. Lin gestured with her palms up, wondering what the noise was.

Jon was about to call down that he didn't see

anything, and then he looked toward his right, at the flat, marshy grounds that he knew the Okalians had avoided on their way to Crystal City. A band of Fens marched along in twos, carrying a platform. There was something on the platform but they were too far away and Jon couldn't make out what it was. He beckoned for Lin and Kyra to come up to the ledge.

"What is it?" Lin asked when she had reached him.

"There." Jon pointed toward the Fens. "There are about sixteen of them."

"They have spears," Kyra said.

"Jon, it's Atun!" Lin said. "He's on the platform."

Jon looked again. Sure enough, the figure sitting on the platform, two ropes around his neck, was Atun.

They watched silently. Jon felt sick to his stomach. Lin had put her head down and folded her hands in her lap.

"We'd better get going," Jon said. "They're not coming toward us. We'll be all right."

"We have to do something," Lin said.

"There are too many of them, and they have spears," Jon answered.

Lin stood, nodded, and started down the hill.

"Look!" Kyra called out.

Jon had started down the hill after Lin, then stopped and went back. He hoped he would not have to see the Fens stop Atun's dreaming.

From the ledge he saw that the Fens had stopped.

"Look behind them," Kyra said.

There was a lone figure riding toward the Fens.

Lin had reached them and pushed her way between Jon and her brother.

"It's the Soo," Jon said.

They watched the Soo move quickly toward the stationary Fens. The Fens put the platform down and formed a circle, their spears pointing outward. The Soo slowed as he reached the Fens, and then stopped within a spear's throw of the platform.

Two Fens moved toward him menacingly. The Soo reached into the rags he wore and pulled out the brass ball. He lowered it carefully to the ground and pointed to the platform.

"He's trying to trade the fire for Atun," Lin said.

None of the Fens moved. The Soo didn't move. Away from them, graceful black birds, their wings spread wide, etched slow circles against the sky.

"What are they doing?" Lin asked.

"I don't know," Jon answered.

"Maybe they're waiting for more Fens to come," Lin said.

What seemed to Jon an eternity passed before one of the Fens near the Soo pulled his spear back as if to throw it. Still the Soo did not move. The Fen lowered his spear and went near the smoking brass ball. He picked it up and moved quickly away from the Soo and joined the others. Then the Fens began to move on, some looking back at the Soo and the platform they had left behind.

"He's untying Atun," Lin said.

They watched as the Soo lifted the Okalian boy onto the back of his ox and started slowly away. As the ox picked up speed, he left a cloud of dust. When the dust had settled, the ox, the Soo, and Atun were nowhere in sight.

"We can stop the Soo!" Kyra said. "We can catch him and stop him!"

"I think Atun will be all right with him," Jon said. "We don't have to catch him."

"Kyra, he doesn't want to be with us," Lin added. "We can't force him to be with us. He wants to make his own way, and maybe he can with . . ."

Kyra's face twisted and his lips were moving; he was talking to himself again. He wasn't listening to his sister. For a while Jon thought he might go after the Soo alone. It was Lin who got them started again.

They were headed toward some woods. This was a good sign. Jon could see the trees, taller than any they had seen before, with green leaves around the tops of their trunks. The branches were mostly bare, but the little vegetation on the trees signaled a warmer climate. Jon felt good. They changed their course to head toward the woods, knowing it might be a wrong direction, but understanding that there was hope in any sign of warmth.

When they stopped, Lin placed a cloth on the ground, took out the berries she had gathered from the night before, and laid them out.

"What have we become?" she asked.

"Become?" Jon asked.

"We are the people who dream greatly," she said. "We, the Okalians. But it was the Soo who saved Atun."

"There will be a time to dream greatly," Jon answered. "Maybe now is just a time to survive."

The Swarm Mountains had been one of Jon's goals, and they had reached them. Lin was stronger inside than she had been when he had first met her and Kyra at the bridge, but she had grown tired.

"There's supposed to be a pass through the mountains," Jon said. "I'll go ahead and see if I can find it."

"Just be careful," Lin said.

When Lin and Kyra had settled in a stand of low trees, Jon started up the first mountain. It was steeper than he thought and he had a hard time going up.

A quarter of the way up the mountain there were signs some Fens had been there. A broken spear lay on the ground near the ashes from a fire. A gourd, its top chipped, was on a flat rock. There was a bag, half hidden in a small bush, and Jon snatched it quickly.

Jon looked, almost against his will, to see if

there was anything in the bag he held in his hand. It contained healing herbs. He was relieved that it wasn't sorpos, that he wasn't faced with the temptation.

On the far side of the hill, Jon could see the terrain they would have to deal with. The green, purple-streaked sky stretched endlessly before him. In the distance, just above the horizon, was a band of yellow that grew into a golden haze before gradually fading into green again. For a moment he thought he had heard Shadow whinnying in the distance. Then nothing. He put his back against a rock.

Off to the south, where he thought the Ancient Land lay, was nothing but haze. He strained his eyes, but he couldn't see anything clearly.

Looking downward from the hill, he could see, against the dark background of the land, wisps of smoke that curled skyward. He counted them and saw there were five of them scattered throughout the area. There were figures moving about one of the dried lake beds. Fens.

Jon went down to where Lin and Kyra waited.

He told Lin what he had seen from the top of the hill. She shook her head and clenched her mouth the way Jon had seen her do more and more often.

142

"We can't go around the mountains, because the Fens have huts near them. We'll have to find the pass through them. I think I should go back and look some more. It'll be better if I look when it's getting dark. The Fens stay close to their camps at night. I'll stay overnight and look again at dawn if I don't find it tonight. Will you be all right here?"

"I'll need time to quiet Kyra, he's very agitated. I don't think he slept well."

"He hardly sleeps at all," Jon said. "It's not good."

"He'll be all right," Lin said. She went to her brother and sat next to him. Jon had the feeling that Kyra would not be all right, not for a long time.

They didn't speak again until it was time for Jon to go and look for a path through the hills.

"Jon . . . be careful," Lin said.

"When I was small," he said, tying vines about his pants legs so they wouldn't catch on the bushes, "whenever I did anything risky, my mother would blow in one of my ears and warn me to hurry back quickly so she could blow in the other or I would grow up lopsided."

"That's silly," Lin said.

"I know," Jon said.

He finished tying his pants. Lin came to him, kneeling by his side. Jon started to look at her

143

but she stopped him, holding his head in her hands. She drew near and blew gently into his ear.

Jon began climbing. It was not as hard as he had thought it would be — there were a few places that were quite steep, but most of it was just plodding along. He held his breath too much, so that the very act of breathing was difficult. He knew he had to do two things: The first was to get to the top and look for a path through the hills, and the second was to find a place to hide himself so he wouldn't be seen when the day came again.

A fog of dust drifted about the base of the mountain but soon cleared up as he climbed. There were comforting, if dim, glimpses of the Red Moon through the dust and clouds. Jon wanted to stay away from the trees. He thought that the Fens would be huddled near them.

Jon heard a noise and stopped near a large rock. He listened carefully. At first he didn't hear anything, and then, from far away, came a sound that was between a cry and a moan. It sent a chill through him.

It began to rain, lightly at first and then harder. He was glad for the rain. The Fens wouldn't want to get wet and it would be harder for them to see him.

He heard the sound again, recognizing it this

time as a flute, the breathy notes rising and falling in the darkness. This time it went up even higher, and then higher still before flattening to the same plaintive note. He imagined the sounds were from the valley below, echoing along the sides of the mountain through the dank mist.

There was another sound, even more distant. It was vaguely familiar, and Jon strained to hear more of it. The sense of it eluded him, but it was still disturbing.

The sounds that he had heard first, the three notes and then the change in pitch, came again. This time it sounded closer, but he was sure he hadn't been seen and decided to continue climbing. He moved slowly, carefully, in the semi-darkness, looking for a place from which he could see most of the mountains and not be seen himself. There was what looked like a ledge above him and just to the left, and he headed for it. The ground beneath the ledge was soft and he took his time planting his feet before pushing himself up. Climbing onto the ledge, he saw it was narrower than he had thought, but from its edge he had a clear view of the mountains. He crawled to the edge to look over.

He could see only one fire in the valley below. Shadows in front of it could have been

Fens, but Jon wasn't sure. But from the darkness the sounds of Fen flutes drifted toward him, melancholy birdsongs stitching the seams of night.

Jon listened to the flutes, fascinated by the strangeness of the melodies, until, quite suddenly, they all began to play together in a haunting and beautiful chorus, then stopped.

Jon was still. Had the Fens heard some noise he had made? A trickle of sweat ran down Jon's neck into his shirt. What were they doing? Then the sudden, unexpected thought: Who were they besides the nameless creatures he had just called Fen?

Minutes went by, then hours. Jon shivered with the cold. His legs ached as the sky began to lighten. He shifted his body and sat up, straightening his legs.

There was the distant sound he had heard before. Not the flute, but the other sound that had seemed so familiar. Now he knew what it was. It was a noise he had heard Shadow make. Had Shadow returned? Jon felt instantly better.

Then there were still other sounds as the world seemed to be waking. The new sounds were clearly the high voices of the Fens. Jon stood slowly and looked over the edge again. He could barely make out a small group of Fens stirring about below. They had started another fire and Jon remembered the Soo, wondering if these were the Fens who had traded the fire for Atun. He was about to look away from the Fens, for a passage through the mountains, when he saw the unicorns. There, held in a roughly constructed pen, were at least twelve of the horned animals.

The fence itself formed a circle and the Fens were on the outside of it. They had pushed sharp sticks through the rough structure so that the unicorns could not get close to the sides without injuring themselves.

Off to one side Jon saw another sight, one that sickened him. It was a huge fire. In it were the remains of a carcass. The Fens were using the unicorns for food.

Jon crouched low and tried to think of what to do next. There weren't that many Fens in the narrow canyon, and he thought that with Lin and Kyra they could possibly avoid being seen if they stayed high in the hills. Jon thought it might be better to try crossing at night, so that Lin and Kyra would not see the trapped unicorns.

The sky grew dark as a small dust cloud passed before the sun. Below him there was a commotion, but he couldn't see what was going on. The unicorns in the pen began to bleat and cry and Jon could see that they were moving, raising even more of the choking dust. As the sky lightened he could see that the Fens had moved the unicorns away from one side of the pen and now were opening it. They were pushing in yet another of the frightened beasts. His heart stood still. Where the other unicorns were tan-colored, this one was pure black. It was Shadow.

Think. He had to think.

Jon looked for markers, something that would show him a safe path through the Fen camp. He saw a smooth boulder, nearly flat on one side, in an area where there were no Fen huts between it and where Lin and Kyra were waiting.

There was no time to waste. There were things to do. Jon had to find a way to get through the hills, and he had to find a way to save Shadow. There were no choices. He just had to do both.

oing down the hill was harder than Jon imagined it would be. In the darkness he banged his knees more than he did on the way up, scraping them time and again on the jagged rocks. His hands were raw and his whole body was aching by the time he reached the bottom of the hill. It didn't matter that much to him. He could put up with the pain.

All the time Jon had been coming down from the mountain he had been thinking of the Fens. It was hard to hold them in his mind. Were the wild creatures who had attacked Crystal City the same people who lived in the Compound, or who played their flutes in the mountains? He tried to picture them in Crystal City. It was difficult to imagine, but Jon knew they would have survived somehow, even in Crystal City.

It took him a long time to find the place where he had left Lin and Kyra.

"Lin!"

There was no response.

"Lin!"

There was a movement behind Jon and he spun around, arms across his chest, ready. The low branches of a bush moved slowly aside and he saw Lin looking up at him. When she saw it was Jon, she got up quickly and came to him.

"What did you find out?" Lin looked up at him. Her voice was flat, as if something was wrong.

"I think we can cross the mountaintops," Jon said. "It won't be easy but it might be the best way. There's a Fen camp just over this mountain. We can go around this one and take on the next mountain. Our people came from these mountains once. We'll do all right in them."

"Good." Lin put her hand against his chest.

"Is everything all right?" he asked.

"There were Fens near here while you were away," she said. "Once early and once late. They didn't seem to be looking for anything, they just wandered by. I didn't know if they had captured you or not."

Jon touched Lin's cheek lightly. "It feels good to know someone is caring," he said. "Are you . . . ?"

"I'm ready," Lin responded.

"There's more," he said. "The Fens have a pen near their camp. They use it to keep the unicorns they catch. They eat them."

"*Shadow?*" Lin's eyes widened.

Jon nodded. "I saw them drive him into the pen."

"What is wrong with these creatures? Why do they have to destroy and eat what we love?" Lin exhaled sharply and clenched her hands together. "How can they be so . . . so hateful?"

"I don't know. The Elders used to discuss exactly what the Fens ate," Jon said. "They knew that very little has been growing in the Wilderness for a long time."

"Okalians don't kill to eat," Lin said. "It's the one sure thing that separates us from the Fens. We don't kill."

Lin turned away and went back to the bushes. She didn't look young anymore. The roundness in her cheek had straightened to a hard angle and her eyes, once clear and bright, had deepened.

Kyra was sitting on the ground. Jon saw that he had smeared his face with mud and had drawn dark triangles, probably with berry juice, on either cheek and on his forehead. Kyra's appearance made Jon nervous, but he forced himself to sit near the boy.

He examined the cuts on his legs. One leg had bled slightly and the dried blood made the cloth of his pants leg stick to his flesh. He pulled it away.

"What did the Ancient Land look like?" Lin asked, when Kyra stood and started walking away.

"Misty in the distance," Jon said. "Where's he going?"

"He's been anxious," Lin answered quickly. "You did see the Ancient Land, didn't you?"

"When the light hit it in just the right way it seemed to be glowing," he lied.

"Good," she said. "Good."

"Kyra doesn't look too good."

"I don't know," she said. "He was really upset when the Fens came near. I had to keep my arms around him. He wanted to go after them."

"Go after them?"

"He found a spear tip." Lin talked to her hands. "Sometimes he holds it in his hands, turning it over and over again. Sometimes he makes marks on the ground."

"Did you say anything to him?"

"I told him that I love him," she said. "But I don't know if he understands that anymore."

"Maybe he'll do better if we're on the move. We should start climbing as soon as we can,"

Jon said. "I don't want to stay on flat land if the Fens are walking around here."

"How long will it take to get to the Ancient Land?" Lin turned to him, then made a funny movement with her hand as if she had been about to say something else and had changed her mind.

"What is it?"

"I'm afraid for Kyra . . ."

"He'll be all right," Jon said. "We'll stick with him."

When it grew dark, they started. Climbing the hill with Lin and Kyra was harder than Jon thought it would be. Not that Lin couldn't climb, but Kyra was bad at it.

The spear tip worried Jon, but he realized that he was glad that Kyra had the weapon. Like it or not, it was something they might need.

As they climbed, Kyra quickly fell behind. Jon went back for him.

"Are you okay?" Jon tried to keep his voice down.

"I'm all right," Kyra said, his voice hoarse.

"I'll give you a hand."

"I don't need a hand."

"Stay close with us," Jon said. "You know we need you to be with us, to help us."

"I can't help you," Kyra said, his face inches from Jon's. "I'm too scared."

"It's okay to be scared," Jon said. "We're all scared."

"Not like me," Kyra answered, his voice barely above a whisper. "Not like me."

They climbed slowly once more, until Jon began to hear the cries of the unicorns. He signaled Lin to stop and rest awhile. He put his back to the mountain and leaned against it. Below him Kyra was still slowly climbing toward them. Lin leaned over him to see the side of the mountain, her body thin and warm against his.

"I see them," she said.

Jon nodded. "The Ancient Land is over there." He pointed to where he thought it would be. "We'll rest for a while and then go on. The sound travels well here, so we'd better be quiet."

The melancholy braying of the unicorns, frightened and despairing, reached them. Jon looked at Lin. There was anger in her face. Kyra felt fear, Lin anger — what did he feel? Confusion? Perhaps the pain of not knowing what to be angry about, or what to fear?

There were scratching noises on the ledge above them. It was the same ledge that Jon had been on the night before.

Jon looked at Lin. Her teeth clenched, she had flattened herself against the mountain. Jon

155

glanced down the mountain. It would be risky, but it would be better than being caught by the Fens on the mountain. The scratching sounds stopped. Jon placed his foot on a rock projection and lifted his head enough to see the ledge.

There, barely a body's length away, a Fen facing away from Jon was trying to start a fire.

Kyra had reached them and Jon signaled the presence of the Fen. Jon put his head down and tried to figure out what to do.

in had said that some Fens had wandered past them the day before. They couldn't take a chance of going back down the way they had come up. Jon eased himself to a position from which he could see the ledge again. The Fen had moved away from them, closer to the mountain that sheltered the small fire he had built. It was too dark to see clearly, but Jon could tell the Fen had something in his hands. Jon imagined those hands. Fat stubby fingers, dirt lining the rounded nails, the thumb set off too far toward the wrist.

There were the three notes again, the sad, mourning cry of the Fen flute. Three low notes, and one high one. Three high notes, ever so slightly different from those he had heard from the other Fen, and then a note both soft and sweetly timbred, like the throaty humming of a mother's lullaby to her child.

157

For a while Jon stood, his forehead down on the rock ledge, listening to the Fen's tune. He had heard it before, from his mother.

There was no way that they could start back down the hill without making some noise and having the Fen discover them. Even if they did start down, they might run into more Fens below. But they had to do something.

The Fen was still facing away from him. Pushing himself up with his hands, Jon crept onto the ledge. The Fen was young, perhaps no more than ten or eleven. The eerie flute sound drifted into the coolness of a breeze and floated off.

Kyra had moved to the ledge with him. Jon hesitated for a moment. He wanted to call out to him, to tell him not to push the Fen from the ledge. If he did, the other Fens would hear the alarm. They would have to pull the Fen back onto the ledge and keep him quiet.

Jon was crouching, but Kyra was upright as he flung himself across the ledge. There was a noise that sounded almost like a loud slap. The sound of the flute stopped abruptly. Jon got to them quickly and pulled the Fen back from the edge, clamping his hand over his mouth.

"Look to see if there are others coming!" Jon whispered, surprised at the desperation in his voice.

He looked up into Kyra's face. It was so twisted Jon hardly recognized him.

"Are you hurt?" Jon asked Kyra.

Lin scrambled onto the shelf. She took her brother's arm and looked into his face.

"I'm all right," Kyra said. He turned away and went to the edge to look over.

Jon looked down at the Fen. He wasn't resisting him. Jon looked at his eyes and they closed slowly. He took a deep breath and tightened his grip on the Fen. He knew the Fens were strong; they were slow but they were strong.

"They're not coming," Kyra said. "Is he stopped?"

"Stopped?" Jon looked down at the Fen, felt his body relax against his own. The arms were soft in his grip. He moved away and saw the blood on the Fen's bare chest. Kyra had used the spear tip.

The Fen's chest moved slowly. He was still alive.

"No! Noooo!" Lin tore at the Fen's clothing, searching for the wound.

"We have to stop him," Kyra said, moving toward them. The blade in his hand caught the reflection of the moon.

"No!" Jon pushed Kyra away.

"He'll get the others after us," Kyra said. "We have to stop his dreaming."

Jon felt his head pounding. Kyra's face was close to his. They looked into each other's eyes and what Jon saw in the young boy's terrified him. The sounds of the unicorns rose from the canyon below them as the first signs of the new day appeared in the sky.

"We'll leave him here," Jon said. "Maybe . . . maybe they can save him."

"We've killed him," Lin said. "Haven't we? Haven't we killed him?"

Jon searched for something to say. A wave of sickness swept over him.

There was a whinnying from below, somehow more disturbing than the others. Jon told himself it was Shadow.

"You two go on," he said. "I have to see if I can free Shadow. Just stay close to the hills and out of sight of their camps. Go in a line with the twin Shan stars. I'll catch up with you. Go on!"

Kyra stood and looked at him. Jon rubbed his arm as Kyra stood over him, the spear tip in his hand, deciding what he would do. He walked over to the edge and looked down.

"Maybe we can stop all of them from dreaming," Kyra said quietly.

"Kyra!" Lin reached out for him and he pulled away.

Jon looked into the Fen's eyes. He was

161

younger than he had thought. He put his hand over the Fen's face and saw the terror mount in his eyes. He pulled the eyelids down. Under his left hand he could feel the Fen's heart beating, but the youngster kept his eyes shut as Jon had hoped he would.

"He's stopped," Jon said.

Kyra looked at Jon and at the Fen upon the ground. The Fen's flute lay next to him, and Jon picked it up. He stood, stepped as casually as he could over the outstretched Fen, and started down the hill toward the Fen camp.

The rain, which had been steady but light, came down heavily as Jon reached the Fen camp. There was a row of huts off to one side. He looked toward the pen and tried to locate Shadow, but couldn't.

There was a group of Fens gathered around a smoldering fire just beyond the pen.

Jon stopped and knelt on one knee. He turned and saw Kyra not far behind him. And beyond Kyra was Lin. Jon looked to see if Kyra held the spear tip in his hand still, but he couldn't see it.

One of the Fens saw him and leaned forward, shielding his eyes from the rain, trying to see who he was.

"Everybody down!" Jon managed a loud whisper.

He told the others to stay put and, half standing, half crouching, started walking toward the pen again. Some of the Fens glanced in his direction, but it was still too dark for them to tell for sure who he was. They huddled briefly, and then one of them started toward him.

Jon lifted the Fen's flute to his lips and began to blow into it. The notes were not as sweet as he had heard the Fens play, or as clear, but the Fen stopped, ran his hand over his face, and turned away.

Jon looked at the pen. There was one side where they took the animals out. He walked to it slowly, moving from side to side as the Fens did. He could see Shadow standing just inside the pen. Jon wondered if the unicorn's heart was racing as wildly as his own.

The walls of the pen seemed less crudely made when seen close up, but the spaces between the branches were greater than he had imagined. Walking along one side of the pen, he ran his fingers along its rough surface. Branches torn from the trees, their edges jagged and twisted, were bound together by thick vines.

There was a chittering sound behind him. Jon stopped and turned slowly. It was the same Fen who had wondered about him before. Now he moved quickly toward Jon, pointing, his voice getting higher and higher. Kyra was near him. Jon moved toward him and the Fen stopped just as Kyra reached him.

Jon turned away as fast as he could. He moved to the pen, looking for the gate. He found it just as he felt a blow to his head that sent him to his knees.

Jon pitched forward and rolled to one side as a huge stick pounded the ground near him. A Fen lifted the stick again as Jon rolled toward the pen. The stick landed heavily across his side, and he gasped for air.

The pain was unbelievable, worse than any Jon had ever known. He lifted his arms as the stick came down again.

Jon blocked the stick with his arms, but not before it had gone hard into his face, and the taste of his own blood filled his mouth. He grabbed the stick and the Fen pulled back, jerking it from his hands.

Another stick, meant this time for Jon's head, cracked against his shoulder. He lashed out at the Fen and missed him. There was another one and another, all with sticks, all screaming their anger. Lin was fighting them off as best she could but the blows rained on them until Jon was filled with pain. Somehow he scrambled to his feet just as he saw Lin fall. He kicked at the Fen nearest her, driving him back.

Jon grabbed a stick that was on the ground and swung it over his head. He could feel other sticks hit his legs and body as he swung as hard as he could. Jon hit one of the Fens across the shoulders and he backed off. Jon started backing away and felt the pen behind him.

Lin grabbed a Fen by the legs as she tried to get up and two of them went after her, swinging their arms awkwardly like ashen clubs. The pen was behind Jon and he looked up to see the vines that held the gate shut. With all his strength he pushed at the vine until, with one last effort, it was free. The gate was open.

Jon began crawling, trying to get away from the terrible beating, the nightmare screaming that filled his ears with as much confusion as his body had pain. He struggled to his feet and, eyes closed, stumbled forward. He tried to open his eyes to look for Lin and Kyra. The air was filling with a choking dust. He began to cough. For an instant the dust parted and he saw Kyra across the open space. There were Fens all around him and he stood with the blade held high, not striking with it as Jon had seen him do before, but holding it defiantly above his head. There was both madness and triumph in his eyes.

Then there was a great noise, like thunder, all about them. The ground beneath them trembled, and they were engulfed in a dizzying swell of sound and vibrations.

Around them, in a great circle, the galloping unicorns raced with a fury, knocking everything from their path. The Fens were fleeing in panic, some of them being knocked senseless to the ground. Jon could see, through the swirling dust, Shadow galloping in the front of the herd.

"Jon!" Lin, her face smeared with dirt and blood, was near him.

She reached toward him and Jon took her hand. As they watched, the circle of unicorns grew wider, forming a shield around them.

"Kyra?" Jon asked. "Where's Kyra?"

"There." Lin pointed a short distance away. Kyra was on his knees, shaking his head. There were three Fens within arm's length of him, but none of them moved.

As the circle of unicorns widened, the Fens fled through an opening in the canyon. Some were injured and were half carried, half dragged, by the others. Lin and Jon watched for a while until they saw one of the Fens on the ground, who had been still before, begin to move.

"Let's go," Jon said. "We can get out of the canyon this way."

"Are you all right?" Lin asked.

He nodded.

Then, as the sun beamed down into the

canyon, Shadow whirled to a stop. He reared up on his back legs and turned. Jon tried to feel what the great beast felt, the joy he would feel at being free again, but he couldn't. He watched him as he led the unicorns out of the canyon. These were Shadow's hills, his own ancient land, the unicorns his race. Jon watched him for a while before losing sight of him in the dust and flying hooves of the unicorns that followed.

"Cheee! Cheeee!"

Jon's heart sank. It was the cry of the Fens. He looked to see where the sound had come from and saw two Fens, one with what looked like a spear, standing at the narrow end of the canyon.

"Kyra!" Lin called to her brother. "This way!"

Kyra struggled to his feet and started backing toward his sister. The three of them started slowly toward the other end of the canyon. The two Fens didn't follow but continued their cries. One of the Fens on the ground, the one Jon had seen moving, started to get up. As he moved, the two standing in the distance began to jump excitedly.

"Cheee! Cheeee!"

Jon looked behind them. He didn't see any other Fens. Soon they would be away from this place.

Kyra looked worse than Jon. His clothing was torn and stained with blood.

"Are you hurt?" Jon asked.

Kyra didn't answer. Jon looked to where he was staring and saw the two Fens near the mouth of the canyon. The three of them watched the Fens as they in turn watched the ones struggling now to get up. The Fens were moving away from them, heading toward the mountain.

"They're afraid of us now," Jon said.

"Let's get out of here before they stop being afraid." Lin spoke between gasps. "Let's go."

As they headed toward the entrance to the canyon, Jon began to feel the pain he hadn't felt in the excitement of the battle. Every part of him hurt. The side of his head, just beyond his ear, throbbed with pain, and he tried to touch it but his arm hurt almost as much and he pulled it to his chest. Lin was at his side, tears streaming down her face, her left arm uncontrollably trembling. They needed to find a safe place to rest.

As he turned he saw Kyra, his face contorted, raise a spear tip high above his head.

"Kyra, it's okay, we're safe now," Jon said. "They won't come any closer."

"It's all right." Lin touched her brother's

shoulder. Her voice was low and soothing. "We can just go now."

"Do you want water?" Jon asked.

"Cheeeeeee!" Kyra screamed and started running across the canyon.

"Ky-raaa!" Lin screamed her brother's name. "Ky-raaa!"

The Fens were already nearly out of the canyon, and when they heard Kyra's scream they ran all the faster. Jon started after Kyra but his bruised legs were no match for Kyra's fury. In moments the boy had disappeared through the narrow opening into which the Fens had gone.

Lin ran after him and Jon after her. The canyon was covered on that side by the thickening grasses of the wood that bordered the Swarm Mountains. Kyra was out of sight by the time Jon and Lin reached the wood. There was no way to tell where he had gone.

Lin screamed, her mouth wide open, her face an anguished mask. She screamed and screamed until finally she fell to her knees and sobbed into her hands. Jon knelt by her side and held her as tightly as he could.

He looked over her shaking form toward the wood. Now and again he thought he saw something moving, but he was never sure it was more than the wind blowing aimlessly through the tall grass.

Jon waited for Lin to recover, giving her time with her grief before pulling her to her feet. She looked up at him with such despair in her eyes that he had to turn away.

"Lin . . ." Jon searched for words.

She didn't speak, but sucked in as much air as she could and started walking forward. Jon watched her for a while and then followed. When she reached a leather water bag that the Fens had dropped, she picked it up. There was another one a bit farther. Jon picked it up and slung it across his shoulder, wincing when it hit a sore spot.

They passed a wounded Fen near one of the huts. Jon stopped and saw the gash in his neck. Next to him lay the speartip that Kyra had used. The Fen's eyes were full of fear as he moved his hand toward the wound. Jon dropped the water bag and went on.

in sobbed as she walked. Her body heaved with each step she took. Jon, walking next to her, saw the skin pulled tight on her face, her teeth bared, trying to hold in her sorrow.

Jon walked behind her until they reached the bottom of a small hill. They had only to climb over its base to be out of the canyon. They climbed together, helping each other as they could. Jon knew there was a danger that Lin would be pulled into the darkness left by Kyra. The danger for Jon was that he would lose her.

It was a small hill and they didn't have much trouble. When they reached the far side, the deep brown dirt gave way to a lighter brown sand and gray and black rocks. Jon stopped at the edge of it and waited until Lin had looked into the distance, to where he had said he had seen a sign of the Ancient Land.

"You knew about Kyra, didn't you?" she said.

"About Kyra?"

"That he was changed, that he wasn't one of us anymore?"

"I don't know that he wasn't one of us," Jon said. "He put the markings on his face, and the mud, but we all learned to survive out here. We took the Fens' healing herbs when we needed them, we fought them when we thought we had to fight. Maybe Kyra just did what we were all doing, he just couldn't pretend he was doing something else."

"I love him so," she said.

"I know," he answered.

"He didn't believe there was an Ancient Land," she said. "He kept telling me that you were lying."

"What's a lie?" Jon shrugged. "I hoped. I still do hope. Hoping isn't lying."

"I think my brother was wrong," Lin said. "I know we'll find it."

There had to be, Jon thought. There had to be some Ancient Land, some special place they could go to and know they belonged, know at last who they were. None of the logic his father had taught him made the idea of the Ancient Land really true for him. There were just images he had strung together with feelings as elusive as sunlight on water. Feelings about needing to be Okalian, and of knowing clearly what that meant. He had been given the memories of a people, and had made them his own, and had loved them dearly.

From a distance the lake looked like a huge mirror reflecting the slanting sun. As they neared it, both of them realized that here was the place they had heard about all their lives.

"Jon, it's Orenllag!"

They walked faster, almost running at times. When they got to the lake they found an area of deep mud all around it. Lin ran through the mud to the lake. Jon followed her through the mud and into the cold water.

Orenllag. This was where his people had come when they left the creatures that wandered through the mountains and had become truly Okalians. There was an Orenllag.

Lin splashed water on him and he splashed her back. It was silly, and wonderful, and joyous. He was playing like a child and enjoying it.

"Maybe we can wait here for a while," Lin said. "For a few days."

"For Kyra?"

"He might be looking for us," she said, softly.

"Let's rest awhile," Jon said. He took Lin's hand and led her out of the lake.

They sat on the edge of the lake in a place where the earth beneath them was firm and tufted with brilliantly green grass. They rested.

What they would have to do, Jon knew, was to stay at Orenllag until Lin was ready to leave Kyra behind.

"Do you think the Fens think of us as monsters?" Lin asked.

Jon shrugged. "I suppose so," he said.

"Kyra's not a monster," Lin said. "Whatever you think of him — and I saw the look on your face when he ran off — he's not a monster, even if he did mark himself like a Fen."

"I don't think he is," Jon said. "But I don't know if the Fens are monsters, either."

"They killed Okalians."

"We killed Fens."

"They eat flesh," Lin said. "They live out here in the Wilderness like beasts."

"Like us, now," Jon said.

"I'm not a monster," Lin said.

"Neither am I." Jon crossed to Lin, lifted her hand, and kissed it gently.

"You are a sweet person," Lin said. "Thinking about building a life with you is not so bad."

"I think, if we're going to build a life out here, it can't be another Crystal City," Jon said.

"It'll be what we can make it," Lin answered. "If we can make it at all. We don't know that we won't have to build another Crystal City to protect us from whatever it was that killed their adults. I want to grow up, Jon. I want to grow up."

"So do I, Lin," Jon said. "We left some Fens in the camp back there. They're in pain. Maybe we can help. Maybe we can't, but if we're going to build something that's not just crystal, if we're really going to build a life, we have to start with something fresh, something good. We have to start with who we are."

"No! We're all . . ." The words filled her throat and she had to force them out. "No! Don't go back. We're all that we have. You're all that I have. If you go back they'll just fight you again.

"Jon, they're not like us." Lin got to her knees, wincing as she did so. "Or maybe they are. Maybe out here we're all the same. But all they know now is that we fought them and they'll fight you."

"Then it's time for them to learn something else," Jon said. "Lin, I'll try to get back as soon as I can, but I have to go and see what we left behind back there."

"I won't go with you," she answered, getting quickly to her feet. "I'm going on to the Ancient Land. I'm going without you."

She looked at him, then turned and began to walk.

Jon didn't know what to expect of her, or of

himself anymore. He turned quickly so he wouldn't see her walk away.

He walked slowly, not at all sure whether what he was doing was right, or if there was such a thing as right anymore. Then, not being able to resist, he turned. He could see her still, her slight figure growing ever smaller in the distance.

When he reached the pass that went into the canyon he walked slowly, cautiously. He climbed the hill and looked down into the canyon. The first thing he saw was the body of a Fen, its dreaming stopped, where it had been before, and, near a small hut, two more Fens.

One, Jon was sure, was the one who had come down from the hills, who had been playing his flute before Kyra — no, before he and Kyra — had attacked him. He was lying on the ground, and the other Fen was kneeling next to him. It looked like a female, and she was putting something on the dark spots on his shoulder. Jon imagined it must be their healing herbs.

When the kneeling Fen saw him, she was startled. She was small, smaller than the Fen lying down. She began to tremble and to pull at her hair.

Jon reached down and took the herbs from

her and finished pouring them on the wound. He touched the Fen's face and he didn't move. He watched his chest; it still moved. The girl's eyes followed each move Jon made.

The Fen was too sick to move. Jon hoped he wouldn't die. He sat down next to the still form. Jon took the Fen's hand in his, and the wounded Fen boy opened his eyes. Using the little strength he had left, he pulled his hand quickly away from Jon. There was fear in his eyes. Jon knew it was true. They had, each in their own way, made monsters of each other.

The rain had eased and there was a shimmering glow around the circle of the Red Moon. It was plainly red on one side, and darker, almost black, on the other. Beneath its hugeness Jon felt small.

They sat in silence for a long time, the girl not moving and Jon moving only as the ache in his knee forced him to change position.

The girl made a soft noise. When Jon looked at her, she touched herself and then pointed behind him. Jon turned and saw a figure coming down the small hill that he had come down. It was Lin.

Jon had never been so happy to see anyone. He smiled and put his hands over his face to keep it in. He looked at the Fen girl and she looked at him, and she, too, smiled. It was a wide smile and her small, uneven teeth gleamed even in the dimness of the canyon.

Jon stood to greet Lin.

"Are you staying with them?" she asked. "I have to know."

"No," he said. "I came back to help. She was here. I'll stay here until it's all right to leave him."

"More of them will come here," she said. "What will you do with them?"

"If they come back before he's well, maybe I can reason with them."

"That's something other than your mind speaking," she said. "Too much has happened here. Just look around you."

Jon did look around, at the body of the dead Fen, at the pen that had held the unicorns.

"Lin, I don't want to go somewhere and build another Crystal City," Jon said.

"If I helped you, we could bring him with us," she answered.

The wounded Fen moved and the Fen girl put her hand on his forehead.

"To where?"

"To a place we'll find," she said. "Or a place we'll build. It could be for all of us, and for Kyra, too, if he makes it. When he makes it."

"For Kyra, too," Jon answered. "When he makes it."

He turned to the Fen girl and put both hands to his chest. "Jon," he said. "Jon."

The girl put her hands to her chest. "Gebus."

Jon looked up at Lin. "I think it'll work," he said.

Lin knelt by the Fen and looked at the wound. Then she went from hut to hut until she found what she was looking for. She took water from the bag she still had and poured it on the leaves she had found. Then she put the healing herbs on the moist leaves and placed them on the wounds.

She moved the covering from the wounded Fen's arm and he tried to pull back. She took his arm again, more firmly, and put it around her neck. Then she struggled to stand.

Jon took the other side and slowly, carrying the wounded Fen between them, they began to make their way out of the canyon.

Lin and Jon walked ahead, struggling with the wounded Fen. Jon thought if ever he stopped he would never go again. The Fen girl trailed a bit behind, stopping when they stopped, never coming closer.

When they reached Orenllag they stopped to rest. Fatigue came down upon them like a heavy blanket, pulling them toward sleep. Jon wanted to close his eyes and let whatever would happen come to be. There had been a time when he would have had to tell himself not to cry, but now he had no tears for such small things. According to the legend, the Ancient Land was just a day's journey beyond the lake. He wanted to see for himself, to know what it was they would find.

Lin was on her knees, her head bent nearly to the ground. The Fen girl had come close to sit by the feet of the wounded Fen.

Jon wrenched himself to his feet. And pushed the hurt from his mind. He went to Lin and pulled her up.

"Lin, it's time to start again. We have to keep going."

The Fen girl was the first to hear the sound of the hoofbeats. Lin turned next, and then Jon, to see Shadow loping easily across the grassy ridge they had covered with so much difficulty. Jon watched him and felt light again.

Shadow was thinner than he had been before, and there was still a piece of vine around his neck. He circled them once, twice, and then stopped. Lin reached into her bag and found a few berries, which she took to him. She pulled the vine from around his neck and threw it down.

Jon watched as Lin held on to Shadow, her face against his neck, her bare arms clinging to him. There was a strange scent in the air. It came and went in snatches, as had the sound of the flute before. It smelled like the sea. Jon looked in the direction they were headed, but saw nothing.

"Do you think he will carry the Fen?" Lin asked.

"If he doesn't, I will," Jon said.

They lifted the Fen again, and took him to Shadow. Shadow didn't move as they lifted him onto the unicorn's back.

As he walked, Jon thought of what would be. How in years to come those who came after them might read about the fall of Crystal City, and about the pain they shared and the long trek toward the Ancient Land. They would read about how they, Fens and Okalians, had together built a city and made it into a wonderful place. And if they failed, if there was nothing to read about, no great city rising on the horizon, no way of being to hold in awe against the starry heavens, then the Red Moon alone would bear witness that one day, four sick and weary souls had come together and called themselves a people.

The End

About the Author

WALTER DEAN MYERS is the author of many highly acclaimed books for young adults, including *Motown and Didi: A Love Story, The Young Landlords, Slam!*, and *Somewhere in the Darkness*, all winners of the Coretta Scott King Award; *Scorpions*, a Newbery Honor Book; and *Monster*, a National Book Award Finalist, a Coretta Scott King Honor Book, and winner of the Michael L. Printz Award.

Walter Dean Myers's travels have taken him to the Far East, South America, and the Arctic. He presently lives in Jersey City, New Jersey. He is a member of the Harlem Writers Guild.